THE ADVENTURES OF CRISTOPHER AND ERICA

THE MYSTERY OF
THE JUBILEE
EMERALD

BY GARY ALAN WASSNER

ILLUSTRATED BY ADAM GUSTAVSON

For Cristopher and Erica.
One of the trees that anchored the hammock came down
this year,
but we don't need it any longer.
The memories are more alive now than ever.—G.W.

For India, William,
Amanda, Andrew, and Jerome. —A.G.

Text copyright ©2007 by Gary Alan Wassner
Illustrations ©2007 by Adam Gustavson
under exclusive license to Mondo Publishing
For information contact:
Mondo Publishing
980 Avenue of the Americas
New York, NY 10018
Visit our website at www. mondopub. com
Design by E. Friedman

Printed in USA
11 12 13 14 15 9 8 7 6 5 4 3
ISBN 1-59336-712-0

Library of Congress Cataloging-in-Publication Data

Wassner, Gary, 1952-
The mystery of the Jubilee Emerald / by Gary Wassner.
p. cm.
Summary: After noticing a mysterious stanger in their small town,
Erica and Cris stumble on a mystery involving the
history of a wealthy family who used to live in their village, a missing
emerald, and insurance fraud.
ISBN 1-59336-712-0 (pbk : alk. paper)
[1. Insurance crimes—Fiction. 2. Schools—Fiction. 3. Mystery and
detective stories.]   I. Title.
PZ7.W2589My 2006
[Fic]–dc22

2005018234

CONTENTS

PROLOGUE

"Come on, baby. Take my hand now. It's time to go." His mother reached out to grasp his fingers.

"Why, Mommy? Why do we have to leave here? Where is everyone? Why is it so dark in the house?"

"We don't have time, dear. I will explain it all to you once we're gone. Please," she pleaded.

A moment later, a man burst into the bedroom with a flashlight in his hand.

"Did you get the cash? What about the cameo?" he asked. He was very agitated.

"Yes, I have it all," she replied reluctantly.

"Good. Very good. Now let's get out of here before someone sees us. Take the boy's hand," he instructed her. "I don't know why you had to bring him." He frowned and seemed annoyed.

"Who could I have left him with? You told me to make sure no one knew we were here. All of our friends think we are still in Palm Beach," she replied quietly.

"You should have left him alone then. He's not a baby anymore."

"He's only six years old! I would never leave him alone!" she protested. "Come, dear." She grabbed the boy's hand.

They rushed out of the bedroom, across the thick carpet, and down the broad hallway to the double staircase that led to the huge entrance hall.

"Why is the house so empty, Daddy?" the little boy asked. "Where's Mr. Giles? Where's Nanny?"

"I let her go. I let them all go," he replied bitterly.

"One day I will explain it all to you, baby. I promise," his mother said softly.

"Put the cameo in the boy's pocket," his father said. His mother hesitated for a second. "Now!"

His mother slipped the pin into his jacket and zipped the pocket as his father watched. Then she smoothed his hair gently with her long fingers. Even under the stress of the moment, she moved gracefully.

"Now let's go!" his father growled. He led them down the steps and across the polished marble floor of the hall.

The beam of the flashlight bounced all around the high-ceilinged room, making it difficult for the boy to see clearly. When the light hit the cut crystal of the massive chandelier, colors danced wildly everywhere. For one last, brief moment, the house seemed almost magical.

"The car is parked over on the side there." His father pointed to a circle of trees by the carriage house, as he flipped the flashlight off. "Hurry up!"

The boy looked back into the darkness of the hallway, but he couldn't see anything anymore. It was as if his home and his past had disappeared in a split second.

His father carefully closed and locked the big front door with his gloved hand, then led them quickly down the wide stone steps and across the paved courtyard. His mother held his hand and gently pulled him along.

"Oh!" she exclaimed, and almost fell as her heel sank into the soft concrete between some recently reset cobblestones.

"Are you okay, Mommy?" the child asked. "Where did the fountain go?"

"Come on, you two! And stifle the kid, would you?" his father said angrily.

"Hush, darling. Don't ask so many questions. You'll only make your father madder," she whispered to him.

The boy and his mother climbed hastily into the backseat of an unfamiliar automobile.

"Put this on," the man said to his wife. He handed her a grotesque old hat, which she placed over her blonde hair, carefully tucking in all the loose strands. "You, too," he said sharply to the boy, tossing a coarse wool cap into the backseat.

As they sped down the long road that led away from the mansion, the boy watched through the back window of the car as the house faded into the distance. The stately rows of sycamore trees that lined the entryway looked like scary giants looming over him, and the sound of the car wheels crunching over the gravel of the driveway seemed unusually loud. The noise echoed in his head and frightened the boy as it never had before.

His father stopped the car behind the huge cast iron gates and quickly jumped out. As he pushed one of them open, young Cornelius saw a bright flash of orange light back by the house. He watched as it got bigger and bigger.

"What's that, Mommy? What's that light?" he asked.

"Nothing, baby, nothing," she said nervously, as she watched the flames begin to engulf the mansion. "It's only the moonlight reflecting on the stone. Turn around. Don't look at the house anymore." A tear rolled down her powdered cheek.

His father got back into the driver's seat and sped through the open gate. Once through, he leaped out again, pushed it closed, then jumped back inside. He stepped hard on the gas pedal, and the car lurched ahead.

"Duck down, Nealie," his mom said to him as they drove away for the very last time.

CHAPTER 1

ENCOUNTER WITH A STRANGER

The wheels crunching on the gravel of the parking lot outside the diner caused the man in the booth to sit up with a start. That sound had always bothered him, ever since he was a kid. He rubbed his tired eyes with his knuckles and stared out the window blankly, as if he was in another world.

"Can I get you some more coffee? You look like you could use it. I didn't want to disturb you before," Betty the waitress said.

The man shook his head, like he was trying to wake himself out of a dream.

"I must have dozed off," he replied. "Yes. Thanks. I'll take another cup."

"This has to be the last one though," Betty said as she poured the hot coffee into his cup. "Sorry, but we close at 3:00 and don't reopen until 5:00 for dinner. It's just about 3:00 now."

"Okay. Can you get me the check then?"

"Sure, mister. When you finish your coffee, just come up to the register. I'll have it there for you," she said, and she walked back behind the counter. *Boy, he must have been through a lot. What sad eyes he has*, Betty thought.

The man drank his coffee in one gulp, pulled his hat down over his ears, and threw his jacket over his arm. He pushed a pair of black-rimmed sunglasses over his eyes, even though he was still inside. Then he stood up and walked over to where Betty was standing.

"What brings you to town? Are you from around these parts?" she asked in a friendly voice.

Betty knew just about everyone in Albert's Cove, and she couldn't remember ever seeing him anywhere before today, though for some reason his face seemed vaguely familiar. She was 77 years old and had lived in Albert's Cove her entire life. Her son had taken over the diner after her husband passed away, and she'd worked in it for almost 50 years now.

"I live in South Carolina," he replied curtly. It was pretty obvious that he didn't feel like answering too many questions. His eyes clouded over again, like he was thinking of a place far, far away. "How much do I owe?"

"Six dollars will do it," Betty said.

He dug his hand into his pocket and pulled out some bills. As he did, a wad of folded papers fell to the floor, along with some loose change that clattered as it hit the tile and then rolled off in all directions. Hastily, he bent down to gather everything up. After putting the six dollars on the counter, he laid some worn photographs he was holding beside the cash register.

"Can I ask you a question?" he inquired.

"Happy to help if I can," Betty replied.

"I'm doing some research for a book I'm writing on a sculptor who worked on some of the estates around here many years ago. He was very accomplished, and there are people willing to pay a lot of money for his original pieces. Are there any old statues still here that you know of? I heard about two horse statues of his near the Village School that I haven't looked at yet, and I saw the big lion at the entrance to the park this morning. Do you know if there are any sculptures of people anywhere?" he asked in a now overly friendly voice. "He was best known for sculpting people."

"Oh, my!" Betty said, and smiled as she began to shuffle through the photos. "You are bringing back some old memories for me. When I was a little girl, we used to hide behind the bushes at the Van Burens' and the Shipleys' when they entertained and watch the big cars pull up with all those fancy gentlemen and ladies." She forgot all about his question for a moment. "Those were such different times. The women were so sophisticated and elegant back then," she recalled with a smile. "Especially the Van Buren wives."

The man shifted back and forth nervously when Betty said that, and she lifted her eyes and looked at his face. *I wonder why he seems so uncomfortable?* she thought.

"Oh, I'm sorry. What was it you wanted to know again? My memory is so bad these days." She shook her head.

"I asked you about the statues," he reminded her. This time he sounded almost childlike. "You knew the Van Burens?"

"Me? No. I didn't know people like that exactly," Betty replied, as if he was talking about the Queen of England. "But I did work at the mansion more than once, and I'm telling you, those were the prettiest and nicest women you could ever hope to be employed by. Gentle is a better word for them. Yes, the women were so gentle... ," she remembered fondly.

"Did you meet them all?" he asked. He seemed strangely interested in the conversation.

Betty loved to recall those days, so she was happy to have met a person who seemed to want to hear about them.

"I saw them all at one time or another, and a few of the women spoke to me in a nice and friendly way, not like I was hired help or nothing," Betty remembered. "But Mr. Van Buren, Jr. didn't like the idea of his family mingling with the help, and he ended up firing a whole bunch of us when he found that one day his wife had instructed the cook to wrap up some of their leftovers and hand them out to us. I will never forget that no matter how old I get. He yelled at her in front of us, and she was so sweet, probably the sweetest of them all. And so pretty, with her beautiful blonde hair. She didn't deserve that," Betty said. It was funny how the memory still bothered her. "She just stood there and didn't flinch or talk back or anything. She had such grace and—"

"What about the pictures," he interrupted in an almost angry voice, and he thrust them in front of her again.

Boy, is he a moody person. First he's nice, then he's mad. Betty wondered what she had said that set him off so. Only a moment before he had been so soft-spoken and interested in what she was saying.

"Right," Betty replied. "There were sculptures everywhere on these estates back then. In fact, the Van Burens in particular were always putting up new ones. They had sculpture gardens filled with statues, but they moved them around a lot. It seemed that they never could decide where they liked them best. I suppose if you had that much money, you didn't worry about things like that," she pondered. "They built this grand, marble swimming pool once, and it turned out that a big maple tree was keeping the sun from shining on it most of the afternoon. So, instead of cutting down the tree, would you believe that Mr. Van Buren had the whole pool relocated? He was a demanding man."

"Would you remember any of the statues specifically if I showed you some pictures?" he inquired, as he started to spread the old photos out all over the counter. "You know something?" he added in a soft voice, bending closer to Betty. "I was told that I resembled one of the best ones he ever made. I sure would love to see that one." He pulled his hat off his head so that she could see him better. *Boy, is his hair bright red—almost too red for a man his age,* Betty thought. Then he tried to smile, but there was something so awkward about his expression—like he didn't really know how to smile at all.

Two kids walked over from their booth at the other end of the restaurant to the glass cabinet in front of the cash register.

"Can we have some rock candy now, please?" Cristopher asked, as he pointed at the amber-colored crystals behind the glass.

"I like the white better," Erica said, and she leaned down and stared through the glass at the mounds of candy behind it.

"Sure, kids. Just give me two minutes, okay?" Betty answered sweetly.

Cristopher looked up at the man, and then he bent over to take a look at the pictures that were lying by the register. The man quickly pushed them into a pile, covered them up with his hand, and scowled at Cristopher.

"Hey, kid, mind your own business," he said in an unpleasant voice, just as the bell on the door to the diner jingled.

"Hi, Cris. Hi, Erica," Cristopher's dad said as he walked in, carrying two large bags full of groceries. "I'm all done. That didn't take too long, did it?"

"No. But we finished our homework," Cristopher replied.

"Hi, Mr. K," Betty said warmly. "What are you cooking tonight?"

It was Tuesday. On Tuesday and Wednesday evenings, Cristopher's mom taught a painting class at her studio in the old village. His dad was happy to be the chef.

"Pasta with meat sauce and some grilled chicken," he replied. Cristopher's dad was a really good cook. "Nothing fancy." He glanced at the man standing beside the kids and realized that he had interrupted something.

"I'm sorry," he said to the man. "I didn't realize you were waiting for Betty."

The man had put his hat back on and pulled it down low over his forehead so that Cristopher's dad could barely see his face. He hastily stuffed the photographs into his pocket, and

without speaking another word, he turned and walked quickly out of the diner.

"Did I say something wrong?" Cristopher's dad asked as the door closed behind the stranger.

"No, Dad. He was acting pretty nasty before you got here," Cristopher said, making a sour face.

"Yeah," Erica said. "He yelled at Cris." Erica was as insulted as if he had snarled directly at her. "Did you see his ears?" Erica asked Cristopher. She made a very strange face. "I think he's an alien."

"Yeah," Cristopher giggled. "They were the tiniest ears, like someone stuck them on his head by mistake instead of his real ones."

"Why did he yell at you?" his father asked, a little disturbed that some stranger would be talking angrily to the kids.

"He was a strange bird," Betty said. "He fell asleep at the table just before you walked in. He must have been very tired. He's doing some research in our town for a book he's writing, and he was asking me questions, but he left before I could really answer them all. There was something so odd about him though." She looked up at the ceiling as if she was thinking deeply. "Troubled is the word I was looking for," she continued. "Yeah, troubled. I feel like I know him from somewhere, but he told me he was from South Carolina. My memory these days is not what it used to be, but he didn't speak like a native southerner. I suppose he was from somewhere else first." She shook her head back and forth and pursed her lips. "Hmpf. Very odd man indeed."

Hearing Betty's remark, Cristopher agreed that he looked sort of familiar. He sure didn't seem like the kind of person who would be writing a book. Cris had stared closely at the man before he left so that he would remember his face and be sure to stay away from him. The guy had definitely been weird.

"I didn't do anything wrong, Dad, I promise. I just wanted to look at the pictures he was showing Betty," Cristopher explained.

"They were neat—statues and things, like in the museum."

"I guess I scared him off," Cristopher's dad joked. "What he wanted to learn couldn't have been too important, or he would have stayed around."

Cristopher didn't say so, but he got the feeling that *he* was the one who had scared the man off—not his dad. *He really didn't want me to see those pictures,* he thought, though he couldn't understand why. They were just a bunch of statues and stuff.

Betty reached down into the cabinet and pulled out a big piece of the amber rock candy and an equally big chunk of the white. As Cristopher crouched down to watch, his sneaker slipped on a scrap of paper. He picked up a ticket stub. On the back, someone had written *49 Spruce Street* in pencil. He crumpled it up and was about to throw it away when Betty handed him a small bag of candy. So he stuffed the stub in his pocket and grabbed the candy.

"In case you have room left after your dad feeds you dinner." She winked at Cristopher's father. "Maybe he'll let you have this for dessert."

"Thanks, Betty!" Cristopher and Erica immediately forgot the stranger.

"And thanks again for letting them sit here and do their homework," Cristopher's dad said as they left.

CHAPTER 2

A PLAN
FOR ADVENTURE

Cristopher was sitting against the wall in the long hallway between Erica's room and the bathroom. Erica was suspended inside her door frame, holding herself up by pushing her left leg and arm against the frame on one side and her right leg and arm on the other. She looked like an insect caught in a spider web.

"Crystal!" he said, opening his eyes wide.

"Why crystal?" Erica asked.

"Because it stays shiny no matter what, and it's hard as anything, and it lasts forever. My mom says she loves it!" Cristopher replied. "If you hold a light up behind a piece of it, it's awesome! I saw a store full of crystals at the mall. They had lights shining on a really big, round one that looked like a diamond, and there were rainbow colors shooting everywhere!" He raised his arms over his head and jabbed the air with his fingers, remembering the flickering lights in the shop. "It was so cool."

"My mom likes it, too," Erica said, even though she didn't really know if that was true or not. She liked to agree with Cris.

"Maybe we could find some," he said. "Then we could give it to each of them."

"Maybe," she repeated as she inched her way further up the wall. "But where can we look for it?"

"Someplace where there are lots of old things," Cristopher replied, remembering his mother saying that she loved old crystal and silver, and that it was sometimes worth a lot more than the same stuff when it was new. He never really understood how that could be. But his mom knew about things like this, and maybe an old piece of crystal really was more valuable than a new piece. No way did they have enough money to buy one of those new pieces that he had seen in the store, so if they could find some, that would be cool.

"But what is crystal really?" Erica asked. If she knew where it came from or how it was made, she thought that she might be able to figure out where they could find some.

"It's like diamonds, only better," Cristopher replied. "It's got more colors inside of it, and it's way bigger sometimes."

"Why?" she asked, jumping down from the top of the door frame and landing on the carpet.

"Why what?"

"Why is it bigger sometimes? How come diamonds are so small anyway?" she wondered.

"Because," he answered.

"Oh," Erica said, as if that was a good enough reason for her. She thought about it for a second. "We can look behind your house!" she said excitedly. "Your house is old."

"Yeah, it is," he agreed. It was the oldest house around. In fact, Cristopher's house was there long before any of the others in town were even built. It had been part of a big, old estate. It had a dark, scary cellar with a door to the backyard that rattled when the wind blew hard, and the garage was like a little cottage. You could pull down a hidden ladder in the back of it and climb upstairs. How many other garages had an upstairs? It was the oldest thing they knew, except maybe for Erica's grandmother.

Over the years, they had found some really awesome things in his backyard, like old Indian arrowheads and broken pieces of pottery and a rusted iron chain. Cristopher had found a colored piece of glass one day that was round on one side and all carved on the other. His mom told him that it probably was part of a wine glass at one time. Once they even found a whole glass bottle buried under a big stone with a folded piece of paper in it. They couldn't wait to open it and read the message, but when they finally got the paper out, it fell apart in their hands.

They were pretty excited now about going on this hunt they had just planned. Neither of them cared all that much if they actually found any crystal, though it would be cool if they did. The adventure is what they really enjoyed.

CHAPTER 3

A BOX
FULL OF SECRETS

The bus dropped them off on the corner near Cris's house, and the driver waited until they crossed the street. Cristopher and Erica walked single file, making certain not to step off of the white line on the edge of the road. If they did, they would fall down the mountain and never be heard from again. Like tightrope walkers, they carefully put one foot in front of the other until they reached Cris's driveway.

"Don't fall!" he called back to her as he jumped over the imaginary chasm and landed with both feet together. He teetered back and forth for a moment with his feet glued to the ground and then sighed with relief. "I made it," he said proudly. "Your turn."

Erica swung her arms around and around as fast as she could, trying to lift herself off of the ground so she could fly across the pit. Then she jumped. She sailed over the ravine and landed almost next to Cristopher.

"Good jump!" he said.

"That wasn't a jump," she replied. "I flew across. Couldn't you tell?" She was feeling a little bit insulted that he hadn't realized it himself.

"Sorry," he replied. And he really was.

The long driveway sloped upward. It was lined with rows of enormous sycamore trees whose branches extended dangerously over the roof of the house. The afternoon sunlight danced through the leaves and lit the pavement in blotchy patterns. The trees looked like long-armed giants standing guard.

"Don't let the light monsters get you," Cristopher yelled a minute later, as he took off up the hill toward the garage.

"Ahhhhh!" Erica screamed, and she ran after him laughing, her arms flailing the air.

They reached the front of the garage and noticed that the door was open. There was a black car inside, and Cris knew that his mother was home. He walked to the back, through a doorway that had no door. He could never understand why the garage had a doorway inside it without a door. But it was convenient in a way. When he came home from school with his bookbag and stuff, he could run right in past the car, and up to the secret ladder without having to set anything down to open the door. Through a window in the back of the garage, he saw his mom sitting on the deck behind the house, talking on the telephone.

"She's on the phone," he said.

"My mom's always on the phone," Erica replied.

"Not as much as mine," Cris said, and Erica agreed. Nobody in the whole world talked on the telephone as much as Cris's mom. He opened the door, and she turned around.

"Hi, kids," she shouted. "I'm on the phone." As if they didn't know. "How was school?" she asked, but they could see that she'd started talking again before they could answer her. She walked to the back door and disappeared into the house.

"Do you think she'll bring us something to eat?" Erica asked. There was always so much good food at Cris's house.

"Maybe." He thought for a moment. "No," he decided. "She's on the phone. Want to go in and get something?"

"That's okay. I'm not really hungry anyway," Erica replied, though she thought that a chocolate roll would taste pretty good. There were boxes and boxes of them in the kitchen every time she came over.

"I'm not hungry either," he agreed. He walked to the side of the room in the back of the garage and jumped as high as he could. "I can't reach it," he said, meaning the rope they used to pull down the trapdoor. "It's caught." The end of the rope had a red knob on it and was twisted over itself so that it couldn't hang down as far as usual.

"Let me climb on your back," she said.

"You still won't be able to reach it."

Erica walked to the doorway with no door and stretched her arms and legs out. She shimmied her way up the door frame until she was over Cristopher's head. Carefully, she leaned like an acrobat toward her right arm and let go with her left. Reaching up, she stuck her fingers out and flicked the knob until the rope fell straight once again. Cristopher grabbed it and pulled, while Erica made her way back down. A trapdoor on hinges that concealed a foldout ladder came down from the ceiling. He grabbed the ladder and extended it to the floor.

"Let's go," he said, and scurried up the steps.

The room was dark, and it always smelled a little funny when he first poked his head through the opening, but he got used to it fast. Erica's head was already sticking up over the top of the hatchway, and Cristopher moved to the side quickly so that she could enter. He sat down against the wall, careful not to stick himself on the sharp ends of the nails that protruded through the wood. Erica climbed up and sat across from him in her usual spot.

He raised his left arm and stretched his fingers wide. "Poof!" he said, and he flicked the switch of the small lamp that was sitting on the floor beside him with his other hand. "Pretty tricky," he said. "Bet you didn't even see me turn it on."

"I was watching your other hand," Erica admitted.

"I know. That's the point," Cristopher said. "My grandpa taught me that," he added proudly.

Narrow streaks of light were coming through the spaces between the shingles and slats of wood on the roof, and they really did make the loft seem enchanted, even when the lightbulb was glowing. There was an old rug on the floor from Erica's house that her mom had been going to throw away, and a little plastic table in the corner with a wobbly leg that they propped up on a book. In the corner, where the roof met the floor, there was a small, recessed space where they kept all of their secret things. To approach it, Cristopher had to walk all hunched over so he wouldn't bang his head on the angled ceiling. Reaching in, he felt around for what he was looking for and withdrew a box about eight inches square.

Erica leaned in and smoothed the carpet ceremoniously so that he could put the box down in front of them. The box always reminded Cristopher of his grandfather because it smelled like him. He'd died a long time ago—at least a year, he thought—and this box had been his. It had the word HAVANA on the top, and there was a faded picture of a big, round smoke ring beneath it. They'd put all of their secret stuff inside that box since they were little kids. They used to believe that it was safe there because they knew that only a wizard could blow a smoke ring that perfect. No one was going to mess with a wizard's box. Now that they were older, they hid it under the floorboards so that no one would find it.

"Let me open it this time," Erica said.

"Okay, but be careful," Cristopher warned her. "Do it the right way. You don't want it to explode," he added in a sinister voice, and he arched his eyebrows seriously.

Erica squinched her eyes shut tight and tried to remember what to do first. She put both her hands on either side of the box and carefully lifted it up in the air in front of them. She pressed the index finger of her right hand against the letter G on the side of the box.

"That's not it!" Cristopher interrupted her. "It'll blow if you press that one first, remember?"

"Oh, yeah," Erica replied. "I forgot. You do it. I don't want to." She handed it to him.

Cristopher took the box from her and rubbed his palm over the top quickly until it got warm. "That should defuse the booby trap," he said. Erica leaned in close in anticipation. Slowly and carefully, Cristopher lifted the top.

"Whew!" Erica said, acting like she was relieved that it didn't explode. "I never remember the thing to do."

She reached into the box and took out the two giant's rings. They were made of gold and silver bands braided together. Cristopher found them in the corner of the dining room floor one day and put them in his pocket. His mom used to put them around napkins, which he thought was really silly; everyone just took them off to use the napkin as soon as they sat down. He didn't think she would miss them, because she always said that she never had enough for a whole dinner party, so she really couldn't use them much.

"Put it on," Erica said. She handed one to Cristopher and slid the other one over four of her fingers, leaving her thumb sticking out. "We don't want anyone to see us." Everyone knew that giants' rings made you invisible. Cristopher slipped it over three of his fingers because his hands were bigger.

"Cover the hatch," Cristopher said.

Erica slid a large piece of cardboard over the opening and

then ran her hand all around the edges of it. "There," she said. "I sealed it. No one can get in now."

"Good," he nodded, feeling much safer. "And no one can see us either." He loved making believe he was invisible and imagining what it would be like to walk around and listen to the things people said about him when they thought he wasn't there.

"What should we use to find the crystal?" Erica asked.

"How about the marble?" Cristopher suggested.

"Okay." Erica nodded her head enthusiastically. She loved the giant marble. It was as big as the eggs that her bird laid, and it had a cat's eye inside. The first time Cristopher had showed it to her, she'd felt really bad for the cat who'd had to give up its eye so that it could be put into the marble, and she'd hoped that it could still see with its other one. She was very gullible, and it really did look like a cat's eye. Cristopher let her believe that for a little while. Then he felt bad and told her that it was only glass. She felt so much better for the cat that she wasn't even angry at Cristopher for fooling her.

Cristopher kept the marble in a little tin box inside of the bigger box. He reached into his pocket to get a coin they could use to pry open the lid of the tin box, and the crumpled stub fell out.

"What's that?" Erica asked.

"I found it on the floor at the diner," he replied. He unfolded it and looked at it in the dim light. "It's a ticket stub." The initials AMI were stamped on it, and there was a small picture of a jet plane. "It's from a plane. And it says, Departure, MEX International, Flight 41, Arrival, JFK International, 5:49 A.M., Seat 21D."

"That's a boarding pass stub," said Erica. "There's something written on the back. What's it say?" She craned her neck to see.

"Forty-nine Spruce Street," Cristopher read. "Isn't that near your house?"

"Yeah. All the streets by me are tree names."

"I bet that grumpy old alien guy dropped it when he dropped his money. " Cris folded it up again and stuffed it back in his pocket. "I thought he told Betty he was from South Carolina." Erica shrugged in response.

He handed her a dime, and she reached inside the big box and shuffled the contents around carefully until she found what she was looking for. Erica pulled out the little tin box with the magic marble and flipped the lid off with the edge of the coin. She pulled out the big glass marble, raised it up in front of them, and held it between her thumb and index finger. A ray of light caught the cat's eye and sent all kinds of colors dancing on the wall.

"Wow!" Cristopher exclaimed. "It's really powerful today. "

"Yeah!" Erica agreed. "Do you think it will tell us where to look for crystal?"

"I'll bet," Cristopher replied. "Let's listen to it. "

They bent their ears to the marble and kept perfectly quiet. After a few moments Cristopher opened his mouth and eyes wide, and Erica did the same.

"Did you hear that?" he asked her in a hushed voice.

"Yup, I did!" she replied, nodding her head up and down, though she wasn't really sure if she had or not.

"It said to ask Pete!" Cristopher said.

"Pete!" she repeated knowingly, and she looked very pleased, certain now that she had heard it, too.

"Let's go ask Pete!" he said excitedly.

CHAPTER 4

ASKING PETE

Erica stepped over a row of bricks that outlined a neatly raked bed of flowers and seedlings in Cristopher's backyard.

"Don't step on any of the real little ones. If you step on them, they die," Cristopher warned her. "The big ones are stronger. They'll come back," he said knowingly.

Erica was standing next to a sunflower in full bloom that was even taller than she was. Stepping up on her toes, she stood face-to-face with the flower. "It's as big as my head!" she laughed.

"We've had bigger ones," Cris said proudly.

"My mom's flowers are all fake. That way she doesn't have to water them."

As Cristopher and Erica snuck behind the garage, hugging the hedge so that they wouldn't be seen, they heard a crash and saw the phone slide across the deck and down the steps. Water from the hose was shooting up in the air, and Cris's mother was yelling into the grass where the phone had just landed. "Hold on a minute! I dropped the phone!" she called to whoever was on the other end. While she was busy trying to control the hose, they made a dash for the big maple tree.

Cristopher reached it first and hid behind the wide trunk. He knew that if his mom saw them now, she would want them to come help her. He didn't mind helping her, but he didn't want to do it right then. Erica waited until his mother bent down to pick up her phone, and then dashed to the tree to join him.

Soon Cris's mom had turned off the water and was talking again as if nothing had ever interrupted her. The whole deck was wet, and water was still running down the steps like it did after a big rainfall. Cristopher doubted that the plants had ever gotten watered, and he suspected that she would ask him to do it later.

"Some things she does okay when she is talking on the phone," he explained. Erica shrugged. Watering the plants was obviously not one of them, but she really didn't care. She was just glad that they had made it to the tree safely.

The backyard was very big. Cristopher's dad loved to work in the yard, where there were all kinds of bushes and plants and trees. Cris particularly liked the bushes that were covered with amazing white flowers. They were called mountain laurel, and it seemed to him as if someone had molded them by hand. They looked like the tiny bushes on his model train board, only bigger. All of them were exactly the same size and shape—an army of plants lined up against the back fence. After a really big storm, the yard would look like a battlefield in one of his video games, and Cristopher and his dad would have to put gloves on and go out and put all the branches and twigs in a big pile.

In one corner of the backyard there was an old fountain that was completely hidden from view by a thick hedge of compact green bushes. A huge maple tree towered over it. The tree was so dense that it kept rain from falling on the fountain. It really didn't look much like a fountain—more like a big birdbath. It was round and made of light-colored stones, and standing on one leg on a pedestal in the middle of it was a statue of a fat little boy without any clothing. He held one of his arms over his head and the other at his side, and he looked like he was trying to fly or something. He had a really strange smile on his face, as if he knew something that nobody else knew.

Cristopher's dad had told him that he hadn't even realized the fountain was there for a whole summer after they had moved in. The trees around it were so thick, and it was so well hidden, that until he started to do some serious gardening, he never saw it.

The stones on the sides and bottom of the fountain were all rectangular, like bricks, and the top edge was covered with larger pieces of the same color. A few of them were broken. The statue embarrassed Cristopher every time he saw it. He thought the boy looked really silly, and he couldn't understand why anyone would want a statue of a naked boy in the middle of their fountain. His mom wanted to have the whole thing removed, since it only got dirty and filled up with wet leaves and rainwater. It had always bothered her for some reason. His dad said that it must be hysterical or historical (Cris couldn't ever remember which) and that they shouldn't destroy it. So they didn't. But it never seemed to belong in their backyard. It was too fancy—like something that should be in a museum.

Fortunately, it was well hidden behind the shrubbery, so they didn't talk about it much, which was fine with Cristopher. He always tried to play in other parts of the yard so that he wouldn't have to be too close to the statue, even though you couldn't see it unless you went behind the bushes. Erica was the only friend he'd ever shown it to.

When they'd first bought the house, his dad had told him that it was very special. Not only was it very old, but it had secrets, too. The first time Cris had seen the hidden fountain, he figured that it was one of the secrets his dad was talking about. That was some surprise! If *he* had owned the house before and had that funny statue put up, he would have kept it a secret, too. Not that he ever would have put it out there in the first place.

At first Cristopher didn't know if the secrets his dad was talking about were good secrets or bad secrets. He was used to *people* having secrets, not houses. It made his house seem almost like a living thing. For a while, it scared him a little. Then his mom told him that everything in the world was unique and had its own history and presence, and that he shouldn't be scared, because only in *that* sense was the house alive. For some reason, that explanation made him feel better. From then on, he'd always hoped that he would discover more things about the house, like secret doors or hiding places. So he and Erica searched for stuff whenever they had nothing else to do.

One day not long after they moved in, he'd seen a man walking around his neighbor's backyard with a small box in his hand. The box had a red light on it that was flashing on and off, and the man was walking in circles and aiming it at different things. He'd spent a lot of time standing by the fence and pointing it into their yard—until Cristopher got near him. Then he'd turned away really fast and disappeared. Cristopher figured that he was looking for secrets, too. He remembered the man mostly because he had hair the color of a carrot that stuck out from beneath a funny hat. The only other time he'd seen hair that color was on a clown in the circus.

Remembering all that made Cristopher eager to ask Pete about where to look for crystal. "Let's go through the swamp," he suggested.

"Ugh," Erica said, and made a nasty face. This part of the game always bothered her the most. Just thinking about swamps made her skin crawl. She hated the idea of things that she couldn't see moving all around her in the muck. If she could see what it was, then it didn't bother her half as much.

"It won't be too muddy. My dad turned the sprinklers off already. We just have to watch out for snakes!"

"I know how to pick up a snake," Erica said proudly.

"Poison snakes?" Christopher asked, impressed.

"Any kind of snake. I saw it on TV."

Erica watched shows and read books about animals all the time. She was always telling him stories, like about the okapi that looked like something they invented in a sim game on the computer because it was half zebra and half giraffe, or the kiwi bird that couldn't fly and looked like a furry fruit.

"What about alligators?" he asked. "There are alligators in the swamp, too." Cristopher looked at Erica to see what kind of reaction that idea would get. It was hard to frighten her.

"My mom has alligator shoes," she said very calmly.

"Do they look like an alligator?" Cristopher asked.

"No," she replied, and that was the end of that.

Cris started to move toward the line of trees behind the big maple. "You have to walk carefully if you don't want to sink," he said. He walked on his tiptoes and took really big steps. Erica followed, imitating his every move. "Watch out!" he shouted. He jumped to the side and heaved a sigh of relief. Erica did the same thing. "It almost got you," Cristopher said.

"Almost," she agreed. "It almost got you, too! "

With another few steps they reached the bushes and ducked behind them as quickly as they could. It was dark back there because the branches from all of the bigger trees blocked the sun, and the bushes were thick. They were also prickly and covered with small, red berries.

"We made it," Erica said when they were safely out of the swamp on the trail.

"If we stay on the path, we'll be safe," Cristopher said, and he started to walk in the space between the hedges and the fence. "The tigers are afraid of the path."

"Why would tigers be afraid of a path?" Erica asked, sticking close to his back.

"Because I put human blood all around," Cristopher replied in a mysterious voice. "You know, like they did in that movie we saw."

"Yuk! I remember that," Erica said. "Where'd you get blood?" She played along.

"I found it," he answered. "It was in a bottle in the garage where my dad keeps his bird food. He feeds it to the humming birds. They like red stuff. It's called nectar."

"Neck tar! Ugh!" Erica made an ugly face. "That sounds gross! I can't believe any birds would like something with a name like that. Did he get it from my father?" Erica's father was a doctor. "He brings home the weirdest things sometimes. And he puts them in the refrigerator!" Erica stretched her bottom lip out as far wide as it would go. The thought of this stuff in the refrigerator with all their food made her cringe.

"Well, it sure looks like blood, and it keeps the tigers away," Cristopher reminded her. "I found it right next to a bag of crushed bones and stuff." He looked at her out of the corner of his eye.

"Why does your dad have that?" Erica asked. This was getting grosser by the minute. "That's too silly."

"No! Really!" Cristopher said. "It said 'bone meal' right on the bag, I promise." Cristopher knew that his mom used it as a fertilizer to make the flowers grow bigger and healthier. And he also knew that Erica's mom didn't grow plants and that her dad almost never even went into his own backyard.

"What kind of bird eats bones?" Erica questioned. "Even bats don't eat bones."

Cristopher smiled to himself. *I got her again,* he thought. Erica was the only person he could kid around with like this and not get into a fight.

They walked carefully all the way around the edge of the yard, staying hidden behind the shrubs and making sure that they remained on the path, which really wasn't a path at all, until they got very near to where Pete was buried.

"Jump onto the raft," Erica said, and she bent her knees and jumped as far as she could.

Cristopher followed her and they paddled their way across the green sea until they got to the cemetery.

A tall, thin rock marked the spot where Pete was buried. The rock came from an old fish tank, and Cristopher used to look at it when it was under the water in the tank and imagine that it was a huge mountain. It was falling over slightly, so he bent over and straightened it. Then they sat cross-legged on the ground in front of Pete's grave.

Pete had been Cristopher's pet turtle. He had died just before school started, and they'd buried him in the backyard in a shoe box lined with pink tissue paper. Cristopher had thought that was pretty wimpy for a boy turtle, but his mom had thought it was nice, and she always knew what looked best. They'd put his food bowl in the box, in case he got hungry. Then Cristopher had slipped a black rock into the box when no one was looking. It was his favorite rock, but he thought that Pete might like it, because he'd sat on top of his own rock in his tank a lot of the time. They couldn't put that particular rock in though—his mom had thrown it away, along with the tank, when Pete died.

This wasn't the first time that they had talked to Pete. They missed feeding him lettuce and having him snap it out of their fingers. So Cris and Erica liked to visit him because it reminded them of how much fun he had been. Besides, whenever they tried to talk to him, it helped them to think more clearly. It was almost like quiet time in school, but way more fun.

"We need your help, Pete. Can you hear us?" Cristopher asked seriously.

"Yeah. We've got to find some crystal!" Erica said.

They closed their eyes and tried to push all the thoughts out of their heads like Cristopher's dad had taught them. They tried to only think about the crystal that they wanted to find.

Cristopher's dad had showed them how to do something called yoga last summer. He'd told them he had taught it when

he was in college. They sat out on funny mats on the back lawn and stretched their legs and arms in all kinds of weird positions. They had to breathe differently and everything. They giggled a lot at first, especially when Cristopher's dad put his foot behind his head, but they'd had a pretty good time. When they were done stretching, he'd told them to close their eyes and try to push all of the things they were thinking about out of their heads. It was hard at first, but it had gotten a little easier after a while. Then it got a little boring. Then it got *way* boring, and they'd opened their eyes.

"Erica!" It was Erica's mother calling from the deck. "Come on, honey! We have to go."

They ignored her for a minute. *Can't she see that we're in the middle of something important?* Erica thought.

"In a minute, Mom," she finally yelled back.

"Dad is waiting for us. Please come now. I don't want to walk on the grass in my heels," her mother said.

"Pleeeeeeeease, Mom! We're talking to Pete," Erica replied.

Cristopher's mom came outside and stood next to Erica's. "Tell Petey I said hello," she said.

"Mom says hello," Cristopher said to Pete. He hated when she called him Petey. His name was Pete.

"Just another minute, Erica. We really have to get home," her mother said.

"Did you get any ideas?" Erica asked Cristopher. "I thought maybe I was about to."

"So did I," Cristopher agreed.

"What were you thinking?"

"I don't know. I couldn't concentrate. Your mom was talking."

"Okay, Erica. Time's up!" her mother called.

"I gotta go," Erica said. "Don't do this again without me. Promise?" she said, and Cristopher nodded. "See you tomorrow."

"See ya," Cristopher replied, and she ran to the house.

CHAPTER 5

WHAT IS A MYSTERY?

Cristopher and Erica were in the fourth grade, and they had the same teacher. There were two classes in each grade at the Village School, and they always got into the same one. They thought that their moms had something to do with that, but their moms never admitted that they did. Their teacher was Miss Shore. She was an enthusiastic teacher, and they liked her a lot.

"Today we are going to talk about something very interesting," Miss Shore said. Cristopher rolled his eyes involuntarily. When Miss Shore thought something was interesting, he usually thought it was boring. "Mysteries!" she continued. *Now* she had his attention.

Maybe this time she's right, he thought. Erica looked at him and smiled. They loved mysteries.

"I'm going to pass around a book I found in the library. It has pictures of our town taken many years ago, before too many people lived here. This school was here, and the library, and the duck pond, but there were only a few homes. The rest of the town was mostly made up of three estates." She picked up a big old book from her desk, opened it to an old photograph, and started it around the room.

"Who knows what famous families lived in our town?" she asked the class.

Cristopher immediately raised his hand because his house had belonged to one of them.

"Yes, Cris?" she said.

"The Van Burens," he said.

"Very good, Cristopher. And does anyone know who else lived here a long time ago?"

This time no one volunteered an answer.

"A family named Magee owned all the land south of the railroad tracks, and the Shipley family owned all the land to the north. But the Van Burens were the richest and most famous of them all," she said to the class.

Cristopher felt very proud, not only because he was the one who had named them, but because his house used to belong to them. And Erica felt very proud because Cristopher was her best friend, and his house was almost like her house.

"But our subject today is mysteries," she reminded the class. "Who can tell me what the word *mystery* means?"

Elaine raised her hand. "A mystery is like something that's difficult or impossible to understand or explain," she said.

"Good, Elaine," said Miss Shore. "We use the word *mystery* to describe something that we can't figure out or something that doesn't have a scientific explanation. If an object should disappear and no one knew where it went, we might call that a mystery."

"Like magic?" Cristopher asked. "Magicians make things disappear."

"Yes," Miss Shore replied. "It's a mystery how a magician makes things disappear—until you figure out the secret of how he does the trick. Then the mystery is solved. There is a solution, or answer to most mysteries. We just don't know what it is. Here is an example." She picked up the book that she had passed around and opened it to a picture of some old cars parked around a huge fountain in the middle of a driveway. Some odd-looking people stood beside the vehicles in front of a large house that looked almost like a castle. There was a newspaper headline in the upper corner. She pointed to it and read, "Famous Emerald Mysteriously Disappears From Van Buren Mansion." This is what's called a file photo. Newspapers often keep photos of wealthy or well-known families in their archives to use when they need them. We don't know exactly when the picture was taken. Photographs weren't dated digitally like they are now."

She sat down on the front of her desk. "A long time ago, a very valuable gemstone was stolen from the Van Buren estate right after the family left for Palm Beach for the winter. No one ever found out who the thief was, and the jewel itself never resurfaced. That was—and still is—a mystery." She passed the book around again so that everyone could see the page she was talking about.

Something about the picture made Cristopher look more closely. He couldn't really figure out what it was, and Erica was tugging on his sleeve because she wanted to look, too, so he slid it over to her desk. She giggled and pointed to the fountain in the background.

"It looks kind of like the one in your backyard," she whispered. Cristopher leaned over and looked at it again. Erica was right! There was a whole bunch of statues instead of just one, but one of them did look a lot like the boy in the middle of the fountain at his house. This kid had clothing on though. Cristopher didn't say anything about it to anyone in class. The statue in his backyard was an embarrassing secret.

"Tomorrow we will talk more about mysteries. But for

homework tonight, I want each of you to discuss this with your parents and see if there are any mysteries in your family that we can share in class," Miss Shore said.

The bell rang, and the classroom started to empty out. Miss Shore walked over to Cristopher's desk. The only time teachers ever talked to kids after class was when they did something wrong, so he immediately started to worry that he'd failed the spelling test or something. Erica waited outside the door.

"I want you to tell your parents something," Miss Shore began.

Uh-oh! The hair on his arms stood up.

"Please let them know that we are going to be discussing the history of your house and the property that your house is on for the next few days. Ask them for me if they have any old photographs or news clippings that they could give you to bring in. I will make sure that everything is returned safely," she said. "I have been reading up on it myself, and I have been discovering some very interesting things."

Cristopher sighed with relief and nodded quickly, even though the way Miss Shore said the word *interesting* made him wonder what she meant. Interesting was almost like strange, and he never thought his house was strange, even with all its secrets. By then he was just anxious to get out the door and onto the bus. Erica was peering in through the glass.

"Okay," he said.

"Do I need to give you a note to bring home?" she asked.

"Okay," he said again, and she walked to her desk, wrote something on a sticky note, and handed it to him.
"Thank you. Put it in your book bag so you don't lose it," she suggested, and he stuffed it into the outside pocket. "Go on now. Your friend is waiting," she said smiling, and Cristopher ran out the door.

CHAPTER 6

XYZ 123

"Whoa!" Erica said after Cristopher told her what Miss Shore had asked him to do. "Do you think your parents have anything you can bring in?"

The bus was almost at the corner where they had to get off.

"Yeah. I know they do," he replied.

"Did you know about the jewels and stuff?" Erica asked.

"No," he answered. His parents had never told him about that. Maybe they didn't know either.

Cristopher and Erica sat quietly for the rest of the ride, thinking about how much better their adventures in his backyard were going to be now that they knew how important and mysterious his house actually was. *Maybe that's where the missing emerald is,* Cristopher thought for a moment as the bus bounced its way down the street. *How cool would that be?*

Yesterday they hadn't had enough time to figure out where they were going to search for the crystal. So today they planned to go right into the backyard and just start searching. They knew that they couldn't dig up any of the flower beds. They couldn't even walk in them because they would leave footprints. His mom was not happy when anyone stepped in her flower beds.

They got off of the bus, glanced both ways, and then ran. Today they didn't care at all if they stepped over the lines or on the cracks or anything. They just wanted to get into the backyard as fast as they could. But just as they were about to run across the lawn, Cristopher stopped.

"Look at that, Erica," he whispered, pointing to a gray car that was parked beside the fence around his backyard. A man sat behind the wheel wearing an old-fashioned hat that made him look very serious. It was hard to see his face because the windshield was tinted and his hat was pulled way down low.

That's weird, Cristopher thought. He knew a lot about cars, and they almost never had dark windshields. Then he noticed the tags on the front bumper.

"XYZ," Cristopher read from the license plate.

"Too bad we're not playing the game," Erica replied. Whenever they went on a long car trip together, they would play the alphabet game with the license plates of the cars that they passed. They took turns finding the letters in order, and X, Y, and Z were always the hardest.

"X, Y, Z!" she shouted. "I won!"

"No fair," Cristopher yelled back as she took off across the grass. He glanced once more at the unfamiliar automobile, but the man must have dropped something on the floor because all he could see now was his bent-over back.

XYZ 123, he said to himself. He was good at remembering phone numbers and license plates and things like that, and he tucked the combination of letters and numbers into the back of his mind. Then he turned and ran after Erica. "Wait for me!" he shouted.

They rounded the corner, and instead of going through the garage, hightailed it toward the gate on the side of the house.

"Hi, kids!" his mom yelled from the deck. She almost always waited for them outside, since that was where they went every day if it wasn't raining. She always said that after spending so many hours alone in her studio, it was a joy to see their bright faces when they got home from school.

"Hi, Mom!" Cristopher yelled back as they dumped their book bags and knapsacks on the lawn by the steps.

"Hi!" Erica said.

"Can I get you some cookies and milk?" she asked. "We're not eating until a little later tonight. Dad is stuck at the office."

"No, thanks," they replied at the same time.

"You're going to eat here with us tonight, Erica. Your mom is meeting your dad at the hospital, and then they are going out for dinner," she explained.

"Okay," Erica said. She loved eating at Cristopher's house. Both his mom and his dad were really good cooks, and there was always so much food.

"Mom? Whose car is that on the street?" Cristopher asked. It had been bothering him ever since he'd seen it.

"Car? Where?" she replied, looking a little concerned even though she tried to act like it was no big deal.

"By the fence near the driveway," he said.

Cristopher's mom stood way up on her toes and peered over the top of the wooden slats toward the road.

"I don't see a car," she said. "Whoever it was isn't there anymore. Maybe they were just lost."

She shrugged nonchalantly and turned around as her cell phone started its song. Cristopher and Erica smiled at each other. They knew that now they could do what they had planned, and that they wouldn't be bothered for a while.

"Bye, Mom," Cris said. She'd turned away and was sitting on the chaise, talking. But the minute the kids had run across the lawn and disappeared behind the bushes, she stood up and peered out toward the road. She looked up and down the street, but the fence made it difficult to see very much. She bit her lip and sat down again.

Erica took off straight for the garage, skirted around the bed with the sunflowers in it, and carefully stepped over another bed that Cristopher's mother had just planted. There was a string running around the whole thing to mark it off, and they could see a bunch of tiny seedlings that must have just poked their heads up.

"Watch out for the flowers," Cristopher called to Erica as he caught up to her.

"I didn't do anything," Erica replied.

"Who stepped in the bed then?" he asked, as he bent down to look at a deep footprint in the soft soil that had crushed a whole bunch of tiny shoots.

"Not me. My foot's not that big," Erica said, and she balanced on one leg and held the other over the print in the dirt. "See?"

Cristopher bent down to smooth the print over with his hand and watched a few of the small stems pop up. He looked up quickly and glanced around the garage toward the neighbor's yard. He could have sworn he saw a branch move.

"Someone was here," he said to Erica.

"When?"

"Just before we got here," he replied.

They heard a car door slam in the distance, an engine start up, and the distinct sound of tires on pavement. They looked at each other for a second. Then, without a word, they took off for the very back of the yard and ducked behind a thick hedge.

"What was that all about?" Erica asked. Her heart was still pounding.

"I don't know. But I think we're safe now. I wonder who it was though."

"Maybe it was the guy in the car," Erica suggested, but Cristopher's mom had said that the car wasn't even there anymore by the time they told her about it.

"Dunno," he replied honestly. "Anyway, he's gone now." He shrugged his shoulders, though it really was bothering him that someone was snooping around his backyard. "So where should we start searching for the crystal?" Cristopher asked, changing the subject.

"Why are we looking for crystal again?" She would really rather they searched for rabbit holes or birds' eggs or something like that.

"Because it's really cool stuff, and because it would be awesome to find some," Cristopher replied. He already had a big rock collection, parts of which he had found and parts of which his parents had bought for him. "Anyway, what else are we gonna look for? We already started to look for this."

Erica thought that made sense. It would be silly to start looking for something different now, even though she didn't feel the same about rocks as he did. They could look for something else next time. "Okay," she agreed.

He closed his eyes tightly. When Erica saw him do that, she did the same.

"Do what I do. Maybe some ideas will come to us," Cristopher said, squinching so hard that his eyebrows practically touched his cheeks. "You have to clean your mind out," he explained, just like his father had taught them.

"Yeah," Erica said and she smiled to herself. She pictured a big broom sweeping around inside her head. "I remember. Maybe I'll just listen."

"Okay. Tell me if you can hear me then," Cristopher said and he started to think. He saw an illusionist do this once when he was on vacation with his parents. The guy was amazing. He could tell people from all the way across the room what they had written on little pieces of paper without even seeing them. "Well?" he asked.

"Try it again. I think I heard something," Erica said.

They both bent their heads down and kept their eyes closed as tightly as they could.

"I heard you!" Erica shouted.

"You did?" Cristopher asked.

"Yeah, you said my name!"

"I did!" he replied. *I did!* he repeated to himself, surprised.

Cristopher put his hands on the trunk of a big tree that rose up tall behind the hedge and tried to picture a piece of crystal in his head, but for some reason, he could only think about what they had discussed in class that day. Images of the stolen jewels and the fountain were flashing through his mind. He had cleared everything else out, and this was what was left.

They sat there for about two or three minutes before either of them said anything.

"Well?" Cristopher finally said.

"I can't see any crystal."

"Neither can I. Let's keep trying," he replied.

He squeezed his eyes tight shut again and let out a deep sigh. Erica put her hands on the tree, too, as if she was trying to communicate with it, and she closed her eyes once more.

"Anything?" she asked him a minute later.

"Uh-uh," he said in a disappointed tone.

Then Erica looked at him, her eyes as wide as a hoot owl's. "Let's look in the fountain!" she blurted out.

Ever since she'd seen the photograph of the people in front of that big old house, she couldn't get it out of her mind.

Cristopher's eyes popped open. *Whoa!* For a minute he wondered if he actually had heard Erica's thoughts. It didn't really matter though. All he knew was that the fountain in his own backyard and the one in front of the Van Burens' old mansion were pretty similar. Suddenly he couldn't wait to check it out.

CHAPTER 7

THE
WEEPING STATUE

Cristopher and Erica ran as fast as they could across the lawn, past the big maple tree, around the sandbox that his dad had built when they were little kids, and through the bed of wildflowers. Finally they reached the row of bushes that separated the fountain from the rest of the yard.

"Come on," Cristopher urged. "And don't laugh!"

"I won't. I promise," Erica said, but she knew that she would. She always did when she saw the little boy with no clothes on. It just seemed so unfair that he had to stand there like that forever.

They pushed their way through the thick bushes and stood at the edge of the fountain. Erica giggled.

Cristopher scowled at her. "You promised!" he said.

"Sorry," she replied. "I couldn't help it."

Cristopher looked at the statue, and then he laughed, too. A piece of one of the big branches that had always hung over the fountain had fallen down. Now part of it was hanging over the boy's head instead. It looked like he was wearing a hat. The wet leaves were stuck to his face, and the broken branch stuck out behind his head like a tail.

"Ugh," Erica said when she looked inside the pool. "Gross! I'm not going to touch that stuff." The pool was filled with dirty, wet leaves and twigs. "The tiles are all broken here," she noticed.

"I wonder what happened," Cristopher replied, as he leaned over and looked. The pool around the fountain looked like it was falling apart. It had been raining a lot recently, and many of the tiles were coming loose. After the branch had broken, a new opening to the sky funneled the heavy rain right down on the boy's head. "It wasn't like this the last time I was here. If my mom sees this, she's definitely gonna want to get rid of this thing even more. She hates broken stuff."

"My mom doesn't mind it. She fixes things, and it makes her happy."

"My mom throws them away, and that makes her happy," Cristopher said.

When something he liked a lot broke or wore out, his mom would say, "When something's time is up, it's up, and there's nothing anyone can do about it."

He glanced up at the boy's face and noticed what looked like thick white tears dripping down his cheek. "Hey! Look at that!" he said, when he realized what was happening. "I never knew the statue was painted. I thought it was made of marble or something." A heavy, white drop fell silently from the little boy's cheek onto the tiles below, kind of like he was crying.

"It's supposed to be made of marble, isn't it? Marble's what people use for statues like this," Erica said. She wondered for a moment if marbles were made from marble, too.

"My mom uses it to make her art. Do people paint marble?" Cristopher asked. He'd never seen his mom paint it.

"We should ask your mom. She would know," Erica replied, and Cristopher agreed. Erica thought his mom was amazing. Her family had some of his mom's paintings and sculpture in their house.

"We should use gloves if we're gonna touch it!" Cristopher said.

His dad always wore gloves whenever he was working in the yard, and they had lots of gardening gloves on a shelf in the garage.

"Do you have any?"

"Tons!" he replied smiling. "We have to go get them."

They walked out from behind the bushes and saw his mom standing at the top of the steps.

"Uh-oh. She saw us," Erica said.

"Yeah, and she's not talking on the phone. That must mean my dad's home."

"Darn! I thought he was going to be late," Erica replied, disappointed.

"She always tells me that, but he's never late," Cristopher said, disappointed, too.

"Dinnertime, kids. Come in and wash up," she called.

"We're coming, Mom," he called back.

He knew there was no point in arguing. They usually ate at the same time each evening. His father was ready to eat when he got home, and his mother was always anxious to get done so that she could do some more work of her own. She said that she painted best during the day when the sun was bright and that she sculpted best at night under the floodlights. On the days that his dad made dinner, he would even come home from work a little earlier than usual so that they could eat at the usual time.

"My stomach is used to this time," he would say, as if his stomach was a person and had a mind of its own.

Cristopher and Erica left their shoes in the mud room and washed up in the big kitchen sink. Erica pushed up her sleeves, but the cuffs were all stretched out and kept falling down each time she reached under the water. By the time she'd finished, her sleeves were soaking wet. Cristopher flicked some water at her face before he was done, and she flicked some back.

"That's enough, kids," his mom said with a smile. "Go sit down."

Cris's dad came in and sat at the table, too. "Hey, kiddo! How was school?" he asked.

"It was fine," Cristopher replied. "Dad?"

"What's up?" his father answered.

"Do we have any old stuff about our house or the land that I can bring into school for a project?"

"What kind of stuff are you talking about?"

"You know—about who lived here before us and those really rich people who owned everything once," Cristopher replied.

"Yes, come to think of it, we do. When we bought the house, the previous owners gave me a folder with all kinds of things in it. They said it belonged to the caretaker who lived in the gatehouse when this was part of the Van Buren estate. Now where did I put it?" he said to himself. "Honey? Do you know where I put that envelope that the Kreegers gave us when they moved out?"

"The one that had all the information about the property? You didn't put it anywhere. I put it in the desk downstairs. Why?" She sounded a little concerned.

"Cristopher needs it for school."

"I'll get it after dinner," his mom replied in a funny voice.

"Thanks," Cristopher said. Now his homework was done, and since Erica was practically part of his family, so was hers. He watched as his mom walked over to his dad and whispered something into his ear. She never did that in front of him and Erica. She'd always told him that whispering was not polite. His dad made a don't-be-silly face, and she shook her head.

When they had finished dinner, Cris's mom got a big bowl of strawberries and a bowl of melted chocolate to dip them in while he and his dad cleared the table.

"Mom?"

"Yes, dear?" she replied.

"Do you ever paint your sculptures?"

"Well, it depends. If I am making something that is supposed to stay outside, usually not. But for inside, I might."

"Do you use marble?" Erica inquired.

"Sometimes. Marble can get very expensive. Sometimes I make a cast and pour concrete into it. That weathers well, and they've come up with paint that will last outside, but concrete statues can be heavy. If you move them, they can crack, and patching poured concrete is difficult. The cracks usually show, and the sculpture is never as strong as it was originally. Once it's cracked, it will likely crack again in the same place.

"You can paint it to hide the patch, but after a while, the paint will tend to fade," she went on enthusiastically. "Before acrylics and adhesives were invented, you had to use so many layers of paint to hide a patch that sometimes the figures looked deformed. Each layer of paint had to dry completely before the next one was put on, and even then, the paint would eventually begin to run." She stopped herself and laughed. "Why the sudden interest in sculpture, kids?" Though she dearly loved to talk about this subject and could go on for hours, she was surprised that Erica and Cristopher were interested.

"Just curious," Cristopher replied, glancing surreptitiously at Erica.

Erica's mom was tooting her horn out front—it was time for her to go. She grabbed her backpack, put on her sneakers, and said good-bye.

CHAPTER 8

EAVESDROPPING

After Erica left, Cristopher went into the den to watch TV. But before he had a chance to hit the power button, he heard his mom talking to his dad in the hall. "I don't want to dredge all that stuff up again," she said. "You know how upset it got me."

"Honey, it was a story. A lot of the houses around here are old, and many of them had histories, not just ours," he replied. "It's not like somebody was killed here or anything. The family just lost a lot of money, that's all."

"But it was so pitiful. They lost everything, not just their money. They lost their reputation and their friends, too! Think of how that must have felt. Our house was all that was left of their whole life. It still upsets me to remember when we first moved in and that person was snooping around the neighborhood, like a ghost rummaging through his sad past. I still wonder who he was and what he really wanted."

"Once we put up the fence, he disappeared. We all worried about nothing," his dad replied, but it had bothered him, too. They had even gone to the police and reported it.

"Was it nothing when that construction company wanted to

dig up our backyard and I had to call a lawyer?"

"That was just a big mistake," Cristopher's dad said. "They went next door, too, remember?"

"A mistake? How come nobody ever heard of that company? Why didn't they ever find that gas line they said they were looking for? They just disappeared after that, and they never even dug a single hole. I can tell you, I did not like those men at all."

"That was a long time ago, honey. Maybe they realized they were in the wrong place, or maybe they got fired for making such a dumb mistake. Nothing has happened since." His wife was totally silent. "What are you not telling me?" Cristopher's father asked.

"I didn't want to keep bothering you about it until I did some investigating on my own. At first I thought it was my imagination, but I saw him more than once."

"Who? Who did you see?" Cristopher could tell that his dad was curious now, too.

"That man. The same one from a long time ago," she replied quietly.

"When?"

"Last week. I was coming home from the studio, and I saw him getting into a car as I turned the corner into the driveway."

"Are you sure it was the same man? That happened years ago."

"I'm sure," she replied. "He's hard to mistake. His hair is brilliant orange. You never saw him—I did. And besides, that wasn't the first time. He's been around again more recently. I wrote down the license plate, but the car was a rental. I called, but the place he got it from wouldn't tell me anything. They said that they weren't allowed to give out that kind of information."

"Why didn't you tell me? Maybe he works in town

48 •

somewhere. Or maybe he has family who live here. If he was trespassing, we should call the police," his dad said. "If you see him again, call me right away. I can't believe that you would even recognize him. "

"I don't know what he was doing. He was leaving just as I got home. But I never totally forgot about him, and besides, I always remember faces. You know that," she replied. "I don't want Cristopher to be scared, too. "

"Why are you scared? And why should he be scared? There's nothing to be frightened of. At least I don't think there is. Has he ever said anything to you? He hasn't bothered you, has he?" he asked in a worried voice.

"No. He never even noticed me. I'm not concerned for myself, but I think it's odd that he would show up here again after so long, don't you?"

"I suppose. But I bet there's a perfectly reasonable explanation. Maybe he wants to move into the neighborhood," Cristopher's father said.

"It's probably nothing. You're right. He must live around here somewhere, or maybe he wants to someday," she replied, but she didn't sound convinced.

"And why are you worried about what's in that old folder? It's just information about the Van Burens and their house, which doesn't even exist anymore."

"I don't know. I just remember reading the things in it years ago, and they disturbed me. That family, the Van Burens, had so much, and they lost everything. Maybe it was just the sadness of it all. I never could forget all those photographs. The family looked so perfect, when all the time, tragedy was just around the corner. What happens to people like that?" she asked, but she didn't expect an answer. "I haven't looked at it again since then. Let me go through it first before you give it to Cristopher. "

"Sure. Look all you want. But please tell me if you find

something in it that bothers you. Promise?"

"I promise," Cristopher's mom said, and kissed her husband on the cheek.

Cristopher didn't like eavesdropping on his parents, but he wasn't the one who snuck up on them. He was in the den first, and they started talking before he could even do anything.

Awesome! he thought. *Our house really does have a lot of mysteries. Miss Shore was so right!*

His dad had walked back into the kitchen to finish cleaning up, and he heard his mom walking up the stairs. Cristopher flipped on the TV, but all he could think about was telling Erica about the strange man with the orange hair that his mom saw snooping around.

CHAPTER 9

A CLUE
IN THE FOLDER

Cristopher brought the whole folder in to school the next day. There was a lot of stuff in it, and he handed the entire thing to Miss Shore.

"My goodness," she said. "This should be very interesting. Thank you, Cristopher." She took the folder and sat down at her desk. "Take out your science books and reread Chapter 11 while I look through this," she said to the class. "Hmm," they heard Miss Shore say a number of times. "Aha!" she said once, and nodded her head vigorously as she flipped through what Cristopher had given her. After a few minutes, she tapped her pen to get everyone's attention. "You can put your books down now," she said to the class. She walked to the front of her desk and perched on the edge.

"It seems that your house was a gatehouse to the Van Buren estate, Cristopher," she said. They all looked impressed—not that anyone really knew what a gatehouse was. "The main house was on the edge of the cliff, overlooking the water. It burned down over 50 years ago. The Van Burens moved out shortly before that." She was looking at one of the old newspaper clippings

that had been in the folder. It was all yellow and torn. "The mansion was too big for their family after a while, and it cost too much to maintain. It was also a hard house to sell."

"I thought they were so rich," Tommy said.

"They were at one time, Tommy. But apparently the son didn't manage his father's businesses very well. Their house was enormous, and fortunes were changing—theirs in particular," Miss Shore said, her nose buried in papers. "They had a grandson who was just a little younger than you are at that time." She held up another photograph. "He was Cornelius Van Buren, Jr.'s son. What a cute little boy he was, but he certainly had an odd smile. I wonder what happened to him," she said aloud, though it seemed more like she was talking to herself.

She put the article down on the desk and thumbed through some more of the things Cristopher had brought in. "Here is something for us to look at!" she said, holding up another old photograph. "This is the brooch that was stolen from Mrs. Van Buren—the Jubilee Emerald. It was extremely valuable, and they never found the thief." She passed the photo around the room. "Be careful when you handle it. It is a very old photo."

"What's a brooch?" Brian asked.

"It's a fancy pin that ladies wear," she said. The photograph was of an important-looking piece of jewelry placed on a dark surface with a lot of other pieces of jewelry arranged around it. On the top of the picture were the words *Guardsman Insurance Company of America*. The pin had an enormous green stone in the center.

"This photograph is from the insurance company's records. All of these items were covered by the Van Burens' insurance policy, so they must have been photographed when they were first insured. This is the only piece that they claimed had disappeared," Miss Shore said, pointing to the brooch. "The Jubilee Emerald was very famous. It was a gift from one of the Russian czars to his wife on her 50th birthday. Mr. Van Buren bought it for his wife on their 25th wedding anniversary.

"The stone has a very checkered history." Miss Shore looked up from the folder and could tell immediately that the kids had no idea what *checkered* meant. "Some unusual things happened to the people who owned the Jubilee Emerald," she explained. "After a while, it got a reputation as a bad luck stone."

"It was cursed? Cool!" Brandon remarked.

"Well, Brandon, people claim that it was cursed," Miss Shore said. "The Van Burens were the last people to officially own it, and it was stolen from them."

"Yeah, but they got a lot of money for it," Cristopher pointed out. "It wasn't much of a curse for them."

"But then their house burned down. And not long after the emerald disappeared, it was revealed that Mr. Van Buren, Jr. had lost almost all of his family's money through gambling and bad investments. He ran his father's businesses into the ground, and his behavior destroyed the whole family. His father died soon after, and they blamed his death on the shock."

"But what is so mysterious about this entire incident is that a gem like this famous emerald could never be resold once it was stolen. It was too well-known, and people would recognize it. Therefore, whoever stole it either kept it or sold it to someone who also kept it secret all these years, or . . ." She paused for a moment. The entire class leaned in to hear what she would say next.

"Or," she repeated, "they hid it somewhere, once they realized that there was nothing else that they could do!"

"Why couldn't they chop it up and make a lot of little emeralds out of it?" Terrance asked. He knew more about diamonds and stuff than any of them.

"I suppose that they could have, but it may have been more valuable whole, if they could eventually find someone to sell it to," she replied. "They would have had to wait a long time though, and even then, only certain people would buy it."

"You mean criminals?" Erica asked.

"Certainly someone who didn't care that it was stolen. The world is a big place. There have been famous paintings stolen from museums and private collections that were later sold on the black market. They can change hands many times over the years. The odds are they will eventually turn up and have to be returned, but the original thieves will have made their money a long time before. Insurance company investigators always keep their eyes on the black market."

"What's the black market?" Mark asked. It didn't sound like any store that his mom ever went to. It sounded scary, but everything sounded scary to Mark.

"It's like a network of thieves and merchants who deal in stolen or illegal items," Miss Shore explained.

The class was perfectly silent. Even though most of the kids had some idea what the black market was, the idea that people in their own town might have been mixed up with it made them all sit up and take notice.

"What about the other pieces of jewelry in the picture?" Erica asked. "Did they go on sale at the black market, too?"

Miss Shore carefully slipped the photograph into a clear plastic sleeve. "As far as what happened to the rest of the items, I don't suppose we will ever know. No claims were made for them as far as I can tell. They may still be owned by someone in the Van Buren family."

Miss Shore passed the picture of the jewelry around again. Some of the pieces looked pretty valuable to the kids, but none of the stones was as big as the Jubilee Emerald. There was a ring with a clear stone in it, and some bracelets, and a gold watch, though it didn't look gold in the picture. They all just figured it was gold.

When the photograph came around to Cristopher's desk, he looked at the emerald pin first. He wasn't interested in the rest of the stuff if it wasn't stolen or worth as much as the stolen piece. He was about to pass it to Erica when he noticed something in the background that was hidden by a shadow. At first he didn't even know if it was jewelry.

"What's this, Miss Shore?" Cristopher held up the paper and pointed to an oval object to the right of the brooch.

"Let me see." She leaned in closer. "Hmm. It looks like a cameo," she said after a moment. She picked up a small magnifying glass and held it over the photograph.

"What's a cameo?" Zachary asked.

"A cameo is a piece of jewelry with a partial view or silhouette of a person's face carved onto stone or shell. It's done in a way that results in the face being a lighter color than the background," Miss Shore explained.

Cristopher looked closely through the magnifying glass at the face on the cameo. It was a young boy's face, and the side of his mouth was turned up in a strange way. He wasn't smiling exactly. It was more like a smirk. His ear was tiny, like a baby leaf on a big branch, and he looked kind of sad. Cristopher couldn't figure out why anyone would want to wear a piece of jewelry that looked like that.

After the picture had circled the room and was back in Miss Shore's hands, she scanned both the jewelry photo and the picture of the family standing in front of the fountain. She gave a print to each of the kids.

"Take these home with you tonight," she said as she handed them out. "See if you find anything else interesting that we might have missed today, and we can discuss it tomorrow." She walked back and sat down behind her desk. "So," Miss Shore continued, "we have a mystery right here in our own town, and we even have a student in this class who is living on the very property where it all began!"

CHAPTER 10

SPILL IN AISLE 11!

Cristopher's mom picked them up at school the next day, because she had to run an errand nearby at about the time they were dismissed. She pulled up to parent pick-up and was so involved in her cell-phone conversation that Cristopher was halfway up the steps of the bus before she even realized it.

"Cristopher!" she yelled when she finally saw him. "I am going to take you and Erica home today." She ran toward the bus, her phone still in her hand. By the time she got to the door, a whole line of kids was waiting to get on behind him.

"Sorry. Excuse me. Sorry. I am so sorry," she said to each of them as she stepped in front of the line so that she could reach Cristopher and Erica. She looked up at the bus driver, and he nodded to her and smiled. He recognized Cristopher's mom right away. "Sorry," she said to him also. "I am just so sorry," she said one more time. Her phone was ringing away, but by then she was so embarrassed that she ignored it altogether. They walked to the car.

"Let me just see who was trying to reach me," Cristopher's mom said. Her phone was her lifeline to the world. When she wasn't working, she felt as if she needed to catch up on things.

"She's been painting a lot. That's what happens when you work alone all the time," Cristopher explained knowingly to Erica. He was about to put his backpack on the front seat, but there was a piece of paper lying there. It was an old black-and-white photograph of a family all dressed up. People of all ages were standing in front of a house that looked just like the Van Burens' in the picture Miss Shore had showed them. Someone had circled the face of one of the grown-ups—not the oldest one, but a younger man who sort of resembled him. Cristopher thought that one of the little kids looked like him, too.

"Hey, look at this," Cristopher said to Erica. She leaned forward and put her elbows on the back of the seat. "That's the Van Buren house," he said, but something was different about it.

"Where's the fountain?" Erica asked. "The one in class had a big fountain. It can't be the same house."

Cristopher was confused. It sure looked like the same house, but there was a big, black car parked right where the fountain had been in the other picture. He pulled out the one Miss Shore had given him, and Erica was right. The fountain was gone. But it definitely was the same house, and a lot of the people were the same, too.

His mom opened the car door, and Cristopher quickly stuffed the photo from class back into his pocket. When she saw the kids looking at the photo she had left on the front seat, she seemed to get a little nervous.

"How come you have this picture here, Mom?" Cristopher asked. "Did it come from the folder in the basement?"

"It must have fallen out somehow," she said quickly.

"So why's it in the car?" Cristopher asked.

"I can't imagine. Maybe it was stuck to my skirt," she said, even though that really didn't make any sense at all. "I am glad that you found it." She placed it in the sun visor in front of her. "You know, that was the very last picture taken of the mansion before it burned down and before old man Van Buren died." She hit the lock button and shifted into drive. "I have to make one quick stop at the drugstore before we go home," she said as she pulled out.

"Can we get some comics, Mom?" Cristopher asked. The drugstore had a whole rack of terrific comics.

"Sure. But only one each or you'll never do your homework," she smiled.

As they parked in front of the drugstore, Erica spotted a gray car in the corner of the parking lot and nudged Cristopher with her elbow. "XYZ 123," she said quietly.

"Yeah, I saw it, too."

Erica couldn't see the man inside very clearly through the darkened glass of the windshield, but she looked hard at him anyway, and then she waved.

"Why'd you do that?" Cristopher asked.

"I don't know," she giggled. "I just had a feeling."

He wasn't sure what kind of feeling Erica had, but he had a feeling, too. He felt it was pretty weird that they had spotted this car again. He had never seen it before, and now he'd seen it two days in a row.

"Maybe if I walk up behind it, I can see inside," he said.

"Why do you want to do that?" Erica asked.

"I don't know," he replied, and he really didn't know for sure. But just like his mom, it was hard for him to pass by things that caught his attention. He wanted to see what the guy in the car that had been parked in front of his house looked like.

"You better not," Erica said. "He'll see you snooping."

"Big deal. You waved to him, so he knows we saw him," Cristopher said. "If you didn't want him to see you, why did you wave?"

"I was just being funny. But now that he saw us, you can't sneak up on him. What if he's still watching?"

"I guess," Cristopher replied reluctantly. But when something got into his head, he just couldn't forget it. Now, even more than before, he really wanted to see the man's face.

"Let's go, kids," his mom called from somewhere near the entrance.

Neither of them said anything about the car, but Cristopher wasn't happy about having to go inside without getting a look at the person behind the wheel.

"Meet me at the front registers in ten minutes," his mom called after them as they disappeared down the aisle.

As Cristopher turned to see if Erica was still behind him, his elbow knocked into a box of tissues at the bottom of a huge pyramid. The whole tower of tissue boxes collapsed. As it came cascading down in the middle of the aisle, a man came around the corner and walked right into the path of the avalanche.

"Uh-oh," Cristopher said, as he ducked to avoid the boxes.

"Darn it all," the man said, as the mountain of tissues fell all around him. He was lifting his feet and trying not to trip when he dropped the basket he was carrying. The contents spilled out and disappeared under the boxes.

Erica and Cristopher started to pick them up as someone announced, "Spill in Aisle 11. Spill in Aisle 11."

"Now we're in trouble," Cristopher said.

"What a mess," Erica giggled. "But it was pretty funny."

They found the man's basket and began to put anything that wasn't a tissue box back into it. Unfortunately, some of the boxes from the top of the pile had split open, and a few loose tissues littered the floor.

"Hey, kids! Leave the stuff alone, okay?" he said in an irritated voice. "I can do it myself."

Cristopher grabbed Erica by the arm and quickly pushed her a little way down the aisle away from the stranger. The man bent down with his back to them and started to push boxes out of the way so that he could find what he had gathered before. His foot slipped on a loose tissue, and as he reached out to regain his

balance, his hand hit the bottom row of some deodorant cans that were lined up along the ledge. Down they came. As he picked himself up and smoothed out his clothing, something fell from his back pocket.

"That's the same guy," Cristopher whispered to Erica. They hid behind a tall display of plastic soda bottles and peered out at the man from the safety of their soda bunker.

"Yeah. It's the guy from the diner. He sure is clumsy, isn't he?" Erica said. They both recognized his voice, and it would have been hard to forget his hat, which he was still wearing.

"Did you see his hair?" Cristopher asked her, but she shook her head.

"No. The hat was in the way. What about it?"

"Some of it was sticking out when he bent down. It was bright orange," Cristopher said.

Cristopher and Erica went back to help the man once more, despite how rude he'd been. They felt responsible for the mess, and they didn't want to just walk away. As Erica picked up a box of tissues, she spotted a small folder with an airplane on it.

"Where'd this come from? It's a plane ticket. Isn't this the same airline as the stub you found at Betty's?" Erica studied it and then handed it to Cristopher.

"It's another plane ticket. AMI," Cristopher whispered. "Remember the ad on TV? They only fly to one place, every morning and every afternoon! This one's for tomorrow at 5:30 P.M."

"Right! Mexico City!" Erica remembered. "I guess he's getting out of town!"

The man turned around quickly. "I thought I told you to leave my stuff alone," he snapped.

Cristopher ducked behind the wall of water bottles, but Erica was still standing there staring at him. He looked at her crossly for a second before Cristopher yanked her to safety. A chill ran all through her body. The man didn't look happy at all. He looked mean. Erica was still holding one of the boxes that had been in his basket before it fell.

"Maybe you should just leave that here. He's probably looking for it," Cristopher suggested, as the man turned his back on them. They watched him rummage through the mess on the floor. He seemed very impatient and nervous.

"Good idea," Erica agreed. She placed the box of black hair dye on the edge of the shelf.

Cristopher slipped the ticket folder underneath it. "I wonder if he's with the guy in the gray car."

"Why would you think that?" Erica asked.

"I don't know. He's waiting out there for someone, right?"

The man stood up suddenly and started to turn in their direction. They took off for the registers in front of the store. A moment later, Cristopher's mom arrived with a big bag of cotton swabs.

"Where are your comic books?" she asked. "I found what I needed," she added without even waiting for them to answer. "I am trying out this new technique in class tonight using oil paints and these swabs. I hope it works." She got in line to check out. "So what happened? They didn't have the ones you wanted?"

"We didn't have time to look. I knocked a pile of boxes over," Cristopher admitted.

"Oh, that's a shame. Did you break anything? Do I need to talk to the manager?"

"No," Erica replied. "It was just tissue boxes."

"They're on it, Mom. It's okay. Can we just go?" Cristopher asked impatiently, as he glanced warily over his shoulder.

"Sure, sure," she replied. "My, what's gotten into you all of a sudden?"

Cristopher's mom paid for the swabs, and they headed for the door.

CHAPTER 11

JUST A COINCIDENCE?

By the time they got back to Cristopher's house, they could hardly wait to get back to their investigation. This time they went into the house first so that they could drop off their bags. They wanted to let Cris's mom know that they had a project to do for school so that maybe she would leave them alone for a little longer than usual.

"We have some homework to do, Mom," Cris said right away.

"Yeah. It's kind of a project," Erica explained.

"Oh? Do you need my help?"

"No!" they blurted out at the same time.

"Okay, okay," she replied. "I can tell when I am not wanted." She acted insulted, but they knew that she was only kidding.

"We're gonna be right out back," Cristopher said, and Erica nodded.

"Try not to get too dirty, and stay in the yard," she answered. "I'll call you when your mom gets here, Erica."

"Okay. Thanks," Erica replied.

She never said that to us before, Cristopher thought. Her warning to stay in the backyard made him feel a little uncomfortable. It was like when they were at the beach or something, and she was telling him not to go too far out into the water.

"Let's go," Erica urged, and they dashed out the back door.

Cris's mom watched them as they ran across the back lawn. As soon as they were out of sight, she picked up her phone.

"I think I figured out who that man is!" she said to her husband.

"Did you see him again?" he asked. He'd been concerned since last evening's conversation.

"Yes. No. Well, not exactly," she replied. "I went through those old papers last night, and I found this photograph. There is a person in it who looks just like him!"

Cristopher's dad didn't say a word for a few seconds. "Honey, that picture is over 50 years old. If you saw someone in it, he must be ancient by now, if he is even alive. You can't be thinking it's the same person!"

"No, of course not. But it looks just like him," she said.

"Who is it? Do you know? Do you still have the photo?" he asked her.

"Sure. I had left it in the car, and Cristopher found it when I picked him and Erica up. I have it right here. The likeness is remarkable. " She was holding it up and staring at the face she'd circled. "It's one of the Van Buren boys," she said, as she looked closely at the captions on the bottom. "It's the one who lost the family fortune—Cornelius Junior. "

"Why don't you show it to me when I get home. Can it wait until then?"

"Yes, I suppose" she replied, though she wasn't happy. "Maybe you can make some sense of this later. " She looked at the photograph again and frowned. *What is going on here?* she thought. *It can't just be a coincidence. I have got to figure this out.*

She put the photo in the kitchen drawer and went to get

Cristopher's lunch bag from his backpack. When she opened it up, she found the folder she had given him on top. She lifted it out and started to flip through it again. The newspaper clipping with the jewelry that the class had looked at caught her eye. She noticed the huge emerald first. Then she saw the cameo. She held the clipping under the light and put on her reading glasses.

What a funny smile, she thought as she studied the face on the cameo. *Why does it seem so familiar?* She picked up the photo she'd told her husband about and looked at the face of the man she thought she recognized. Standing beside him was a beautiful woman who almost looked as if she was trying to hide. She was looking down at a small boy whose hand she held, and her shadow partly covered his face. He was wearing a little cap with a button on the top and a small brim. He couldn't have been more than five or six.

His face looks a lot like the child on the cameo, she thought. *They have the same tiny ears. But all these men look remarkably alike. I wish I could see him more clearly.*

She thought about it for a moment more. Then she reluctantly put everything back in the folder, closed it, and slipped it back into Cristopher's pack.

CHAPTER 12

A SURPRISING DISCOVERY

"Let's get the gloves," Cristopher said as he jumped down the four steps from the deck to the lawn all at once.

Erica followed him into the side door of the garage and watched as he dragged a small ladder over to the shelves that lined the back wall. He climbed up and started throwing things down to her.

"Catch," he called.

Erica caught the first thing that he threw, but the second one hit her in the arm as she was reaching for the first one, and when she bent down to pick up the second one, a third thing hit her in the head.

"Hey!" she protested. "I can't catch that fast!"

By the time Cristopher had climbed down the ladder, Erica had put on a pair of black rubber gloves and was holding a pair of green garden gloves. The black ones reached almost to her shoulders. The fingers were so long and wide that she could put more than one of her own in each space.

"Here," she said, handing the green ones to Cristopher.

"Let's go!" He dashed out the door with Erica close at his heels.

They ran all the way to the fountain. This time the statue had wet leaves stuck to it in a number of places, but the boy's head was no longer covered. A bird that had been sitting on his shoulder took off as they ran up, and Erica watched it fly to a nearby branch.

"It's watching us," she said to Cristopher. "Do you think it's really a bird?" she kidded.

"I don't know. I hope so," he replied, more seriously than she expected.

"So do I," Erica said. She didn't like the way the bird was staring at them. "I think it's a spy, " she concluded. She picked up a small stone and tossed it near the bird, but it didn't move. "See? It's a spy for sure. "

Cristopher picked up a broken branch from inside the fountain's pool and threw it. This time, the bird flew away.

"Come on in, the water's fine!" Cristopher teased.

Erica climbed up the stones and carefully stepped down into the fountain. The inside was covered with wet leaves and twigs.

"What are we looking for exactly?" Erica asked.

"A secret place," Cristopher answered her. "Somewhere that you could hide something. You know, like a treasure."

He was picking up wads of wet leaves and heaving them out of the fountain.

"Yuk!" Erica said. "These smell." She made a face as she threw a handful over the edge.

Once they had cleared out most of the leaves and other debris, they got down on all fours and started to look more closely at the bricks on the bottom, each of them moving in opposite directions around the statue.

"I don't see anything," Erica said. "All the tiles look the same. "

"Keep looking," Cristopher replied. He lifted up a particularly large wad of wet, slimy leaves and noticed that his glove was covered with a white substance. "Look at this!"

"What? Did you find something!" she asked excitedly.

"No," he replied. "But my gloves are all full of white stuff!"

"It looks like paint," she said, standing up on the outside edge of the pool. "It's dripping from all over the statue now—it looks like he's starting to melt or something!"

Cristopher looked up at the boy's face from directly underneath. Then he climbed up on the edge of the fountain so that he was a little higher up and stared at the statue.

"What are you looking for now?" Erica asked.

"I don't know," Cristopher replied very seriously, as he walked all around the statue. Without taking his eyes off of the boy, he asked, "Does he look like somebody you know?"

Erica stood up and stared. "No," she said finally.

Cristopher looked perplexed. He climbed down and started to search the bottom of the fountain again for a trap-door or a secret hiding place. Something told him that this was no ordinary fountain. The fact that the statue seemed to be painted with lots of layers, as his mom said, was weird. Erica jumped in and began to search again as well.

Their knees were sopping wet by the time they made their way from one side to the other, pressing on bricks and examining them as closely as they could. Every once in a while Cristopher would pound on a stone with his hand and then move on to another one. Erica's gloves were flopping all over the place and her face was streaked with mud. Cristopher glanced over at her from the other side of the fountain and laughed.

They searched a little longer, until their paths met at the place where they had started. Cristopher slid backward and sat with his back propped up against the pedestal in the middle of the fountain. A minute later, Erica joined him, sighing exactly the way her mother did when her father called to say he'd be late for dinner again.

"Maybe there's really nothing here," Erica said.

"Maybe," Cristopher agreed, but he was disappointed with that thought. And he was frustrated. There were supposed to be secret hiding places in old statues and stuff like this!

"Hey! I know where I saw him before!" Cristopher almost shouted, startling Erica.

"Who?" Erica asked as she pulled the muddy gloves from her hands.

"The statue! He looks like that kid on the cameo pin!" he said. "Look at those ears. How many people have ears that small?"

"This kid looks like an otter," Erica laughed. "They have little ears, too."

Cristopher stood up and cocked his head to the side so he could look at the face of the statue in profile against the dark green of the trees. Then Erica started to climb onto the top of the pedestal. Once she was sitting on the platform, she decided that she could get a better look if she climbed right up on top of the statue. Whenever there was something to climb, it was hard for her to resist, and this time she had a good reason to get closer.

"You think they look alike?" she asked Cristopher. "I don't remember what the cameo looked like." Erica threw her arm across the boy's back and tried to swing her leg over the top like she would if she were getting on a pony, but she couldn't find anything to grab hold of. Finally she chose the back leg. She was starting to pull herself up when she heard a dull cracking noise.

"Uh-oh!" she said, as the leg broke off at the knee and fell into the fountain right next to Cristopher.

Cristopher stood up and looked at Erica. Then he looked at the broken statue and once more at the piece of the leg lying in the fountain.

"Uh-oh!" he repeated.

Erica climbed down and picked up the leg. It was much lighter than she expected it to be. The cement covered a web of chicken wire mesh, so the leg was basically hollow. The end

where it had broken off was covered with thick, sticky paint.

"Do you think we can glue it back on?" she asked, knowing perfectly well that it was too heavy for plain glue. "What are we gonna do?"

She was getting more and more worried, and Cristopher was not helping at all. In fact, he didn't even seem to care.

Cristopher turned to look at Erica. "It's the same face for sure!" he almost shouted at her. "Look at him. That's the kid in the picture Miss Shore passed around, too!"

What he was saying didn't register right away. Erica was too busy wondering how much trouble she was going to be in for breaking the statue's leg. She put the dismembered leg down and went and stood next to Cristopher. Suddenly, she realized what he was talking about.

"You're right!" she gasped a moment later. She was staring at the statue, and her eyes were as wide as Cristopher's. "Wow! This is awesome! But what a dumb smile he has."

"It's not dumb. It's sad," Cristopher said. "It's like he knows a secret, and it's making him unhappy or something." Then they looked at each other, and their jaws dropped. "Maybe we found the secret place!" he whispered, more surprised than he had ever been in his whole life. They scrambled onto the pedestal and started to examine the statue more closely.

"Look here!" Cristopher shouted. He was looking into the hole in the statue's broken leg. He pushed his hand deep inside and tried to pull something out, but he still had the glove on, so his hand got stuck. "I think I found something, but I can't get my arm out!"

Erica pulled her gloves off and tried to help, but even together they couldn't get his hand out. "You have to pull your hand out of the glove," she said, realizing that this was the only way he was ever going to get free.

Cristopher extricated his hand, leaving the end of the glove sticking out from the broken knee. Then he jumped down and took off across the backyard with Erica in hot pursuit. He flung open the garage door and grabbed a pair of long pliers off of his father's tool wall. So as not to be empty-handed, Erica picked up a pair of tongs that Cristopher's father used for their barbecue and dashed out the door behind Cristopher.

Back at the statue, they climbed up on the base and stuck their tools into the opening, grabbing whatever bit of the glove they could latch onto.

"Pull!" Erica said, and they yanked as hard as they could. The glove came sailing out of the broken knee joint and, along with the tools, fell with a thud onto the bricks below.

Cristopher and Erica could see something sticking out from a nest of moldy straw in the space where the glove had been wedged only moments before. Cristopher reached up and yanked an oddly shaped box tied up with string from its hiding place.

CHAPTER 13

NOW WHAT DO WE DO?

Cristopher and Erica made a mad dash for their secret hideout, in the garage, so excited that they could barely contain themselves. Cristopher turned the light on and put the box down in the middle of the carpet.

"Should we open it? What do you think it is?" Erica asked.

"We won't know until we look," Cristopher replied. "Do you want to do it? You found the hiding place."

"Let's do it together."

They lifted up the box and started to pull off the string. But it was so old that it fell apart almost as soon as they touched it. Erica held the bottom of the box while Cristopher lifted the cover. They were staring at it so intently that their eyes hurt. Inside of the box was a black velvet pouch that looked extremely old.

"Do you think it's boobytrapped?" Cristopher asked, and this time he was serious.

"No way," Erica replied. "No one was supposed to find it, so why would it be?" That seemed logical, so Cristopher didn't waste another moment. He gently lifted the pouch out and placed it on the floor in front of them.

"It's really soft," Cristopher murmured. A string was pulled tight and knotted at the top. Once the knot was loose, he was able to pull open the pouch. Then he turned it over and dumped the contents on the carpet.

Erica gasped. Cristopher could hardly make a sound. They looked at each other, then at the object, then at each other again. Lying on the carpet was the missing brooch. The Jubilee Emerald sparkled wildly in the light of their tiny lamp.

It was a few moments before either could speak. Finally Cristopher picked up the brooch and looked at it closely. Then he handed it to Erica—carefully, as if it might break.

"This is *way* better than crystal!" he finally said.

"Way better!" Erica agreed, nodding her head like a bobble doll and smiling. Then her smile disappeared completely, and she looked frightened. "What do we do now?" she asked. "What if the person who stole it comes back for it? Or what if some black market people are trying to find it?"

Cristopher hadn't thought about that. He hadn't thought about anything else at all since they had found the box.

"That was a really long time ago," he said, but suddenly he was a little nervous. And he hadn't even told Erica what he'd overheard his parents talking about the other day. "We should keep it a secret," he said, and he looked at Erica with his eyes wide. "That guy's looking for it, too!" he whispered.

"What guy?" Erica asked.

"The one in the diner with the pictures. The one with the red hair and the hat and the hair dye! The one in the drugstore!"

"How do you know? Are you sure?" she asked. Then another thought occurred to her. "Uh-oh. And he saw me!" She was getting more worried. "And so did the man in the gray car! You think they're partners?"

"The one from the drugstore's been snooping around here for a while," Cristopher said. "I saw him in the yard next door a

long time ago. When he saw me, he ran away. My mom has seen him, too. And we saw the gray car out front the other day. I bet this is why!" They stared down at the glittering emerald brooch. "And what about the footprint in my mom's flower bed? It wasn't yours, and it wasn't mine, and my dad would never step on my mom's seedlings."

"Yeah!" Erica agreed. "That means he was here."

"Yeah! And not long ago," Cristopher added uneasily.

"Do you think he's a robber?" Erica asked, meaning the man from the drugstore. "I don't like his eyes. He looks shifty."

Cristopher didn't answer right away. He was thinking. "Wow, Erica!" he said and looked right at her like something else amazing had just happened.

"What?" she asked. "What's the matter now?"

"You said it!" Cristopher replied, but Erica didn't know what he was talking about. "His eyes!" Cristopher reminded her. "They looked shifty, like he knew some big secret. Just like the kid on the cameo!"

"And just like the boy on the statue!" she said. It felt as if a lightbulb had snapped on inside her head.

"And he had otter ears!" Cristopher practically shouted.

They stood there in total silence for a moment.

"So what do we do now?" Erica finally asked.

"We have to hide it until we figure out what to do with it. We shouldn't tell anyone!"

"No one!" she repeated.

"What about the curse?" Cristopher remembered. "Do you think we'll get it?" he asked, as if it was like the chicken pox.

"Uh-uh," Erica said seriously after thinking about it for a moment. "We're not going to keep the emerald. The curse won't get us if we don't keep it."

Cristopher was satisfied with that answer. It seemed to make sense. Maybe only people who had owned it before or wanted to own it got cursed by it.

Erica picked up the pin, put it back in the pouch, and then put the pouch back into the box. Cristopher put the cover on the box and picked the whole thing up. He put it in their secret hiding place in the corner and came back and sat down.

"No one will ever find it up here," Erica said, but she wasn't so sure anymore. "Will they?" Their make-believe booby traps weren't going to keep a real live robber away. Suddenly, she wished that they really could do some of the things that they pretended they could do.

"I'm gonna come up here in the morning and get it before the bus comes. It should be safe here until morning," he said. "I don't want to sleep with it in my room! I'll bring it to school tomorrow and keep it hidden. We can't leave it here. What if one of those men come looking for it again?"

"No way can we leave it here, and no way would I want it in my room either!" Erica completely agreed with him. If it was in her room, she would never be able to sleep. Just the thought of it made her shudder. "You won't be scared tomorrow?"

"I will, but I'll do it," Cristopher replied. Erica knew that he would. "Let's go," he said.

"What about the gloves?" Erica suddenly remembered. "What if your dad needs them? If he does, and he can't find them, he may start asking you stuff."

"He won't need them before the weekend. I'll get them after school. There's no way I'm going back there now!" he said referring to the fountain, and Erica nodded. She agreed totally.

He flipped off the light, but this time, before he climbed down the ladder, he stuck his head partway out of the hatch and looked around, just to be safe. When he was sure no one was there, he motioned to Erica to follow him down. They were anxious to get out of the garage and into the house.

Cristopher peered through the glass of the door, almost

expecting to see a face glaring back at him. Fortunately no one was there. He pushed open the door to the backyard just a little bit, stuck his head out partway, and looked in both directions before stepping outside. Together he and Erica dashed to the safety of the deck.

CHAPTER 14

HOT
ON THE TRAIL

The next morning, before the bus came to pick him up, Cristopher stepped out onto the deck, looked all around the backyard, then ran as fast as he could to the side door of the garage. He glanced first to the left and then to the right before pushing the door open and ducking in behind it. He pulled it shut and flipped the lock. Cristopher had never locked the door before when he was in the garage, but today was different. He could feel his heart pounding.

As quickly as he could, he grabbed the rope and pulled the ladder down. Then Cristopher raced up the steps without turning on any lights and snatched the box from its hiding place. Pulling out the velvet pouch, he dropped the empty box on the floor and scurried back down the ladder. The whole thing couldn't have taken more than two minutes. He stuffed the pouch into his pocket and was about to run back to the house when he stepped on something soft. He looked down and saw that he was standing on one of the gloves he'd left in the fountain the day before.

How did that get here? Cristopher got goose bumps all over. *Someone was in the garage!* he realized immediately. Without another thought, he tore off to his house as fast as he could, just as the bus was pulling up. No one seemed to notice how out of breath he was—except for Erica, who didn't have to ask why.

Once in class, Cristopher and Erica could barely speak. Miss Shore was starting to look at the two of them strangely, partly because of how quiet they seemed, but also because they were acting as if they were sharing some big secret, which, of course they were! The pouch in Cristopher's pocket was poking into his thigh. He couldn't wait for math to end so that they could go out for recess.

"Okay, you can pass in your workbooks," Miss Shore finally said. She erased what she had written on the board and walked to the front of her desk. "After recess we will continue our discussion about the mystery of the missing brooch. " Everyone headed for the door.

Erica and Cristopher dashed down the steps and out the big double doors. In the very back of the school yard was a spot sheltered by thick trees that they used as a kind of clubhouse. They could sit there and talk, and try to figure out what to do with the brooch. Cristopher certainly didn't want to have to carry it around in his pocket forever. As they were running down the path that abutted the bus circle in front of the school, they saw someone standing next to the horse sculpture.

"Duck!" Cristopher said urgently. "That's him!" He grabbed Erica's arm and pulled her down behind a bush. "Do you see him?"

"Yeah! What's he doing?" she asked, as they stared at the man through the branches.

"I bet he's trying to find the emerald. Maybe he thinks it's hidden in one of the horses somewhere."

"He sure seems nervous," Erica replied.

As they watched, they heard his cell phone ring. He pulled it out of his pocket and looked around suspiciously before he began talking.

"I told you, I'll have it soon! But . . . but . . .," he stammered into the phone as he wiped his forehead with a handkerchief. "*I know* you paid me for it, but I just gave you that other bracelet last month. I wouldn't have stolen that one if I thought you were going to keep threatening me about this. I would've kept it for myself!" He moved the phone an inch or two from his ear as if the person on the other end was yelling at him. "We'll *all* go to jail if you do that. I am not taking the fall alone. You got most of that insurance money anyway, and you still have the jewelry! If I go down, you're going with me. I only kept a hundred thousand. You walked off with half a million!" He made a sour face. "Listen, if I want to gamble, that's my business. Don't go telling me what to . . ."

Suddenly a car door slammed in the distance, and he stopped in mid-sentence, as if he had just remembered that he was standing in the middle of a school parking lot. His eyes darted from left to right. "I gotta go. Give me another day. Just one more day, that's all I ask. I swear I'll bring it to Miami myself by tomorrow night. I already got my plane ticket. Trust me," he said, and slipped the phone into his pocket.

"Trust him? Yeah, sure," Cristopher whispered. "He's not going to Miami with that ticket. What a liar!"

"He's leaving," Erica said as they watched closely. "He's walking toward the street."

They knew immediately what they had to do. "Let's go," Cristopher said. Making sure to stay well hidden, they followed him out the gates and down the narrow lane that led toward Erica's cul-de-sac.

"Where do you think he's going? To my house?" " she asked nervously.

Cristopher looked up at the street sign on the corner right

next to him. "Forty-nine Spruce Street!" Cristopher replied, without any doubt in his voice.

When they reached the house with 49 on the mailbox, they stepped into the booth where people waited for the bus, making sure they couldn't be seen by anyone at the house. They waited impatiently for about 10 minutes and took turns watching the door.

"Who lives there, do you think?" Erica asked as they switched positions.

"Watch," Cristopher said as a young man followed the red-haired guy out the door and onto the stoop.

"And don't bother us again!" the young man said angrily, practically pushing him down the front steps. "My grandfather's an old man with a weak heart. You shouldn't go threatening him like that. He's been a bona fide American citizen for almost 30 years now, so just leave us alone. I'm warning you! I'll call the police if you don't leave now. I may just do that anyway!" Then the young man walked back inside and slammed the door.

The red-haired man walked briskly away, heading for a car that was parked a short way up the street.

"We better get back to school. We shouldn't even be here," Erica said.

"I know. But I have to talk to him!" Cristopher meant the young man who had just walked back inside his house. "You can go back if you want to."

"No way! I'm coming with you," Erica replied. As soon as the red-haired man's car had driven up the street and out of sight, they dashed for the front door of 49 Spruce Street and rang the bell.

"Can I help you?" the young man asked after opening the door. He was looking around suspiciously, as if he expected the other guy to come back.

"Sorry to bother you, but can you tell us what that man who

just left here wanted?" Cristopher asked.

"Why? What's it to you?" he asked warily.

"He's been snooping around my house, and we heard you argue with him," Cristopher replied. "He scared my mom."

That seemed to put the man at ease. "I've seen you around this neighborhood, haven't I?" he asked Erica, and she nodded in response. "I suppose it's okay to tell you then," he said.

"My grandfather used to work for a family named Van Buren a long time ago. He was one of their gardeners. This guy wanted to talk to him about some dumb statue or something that used to be on their property. I don't know who he is or why he cares, but he seemed kind of desperate. He was very nervous," the young man explained. "When I wouldn't let him in, he threatened me and said he was going to report my grandpa to the Department of Immigration and Naturalization for being here illegally. Sure, 50 years ago he came here illegally, but he applied for citizenship as soon as they had an amnesty program. He's got nothing to be afraid of now."

Erica looked at Cristopher and raised her eyebrows knowingly.

"I told him that if he bothers us again, I'm going to call the police. He kept looking at his watch the whole time—like he was in a really big hurry, like he had to catch a train or something," the young man said.

"More like a plane," Cristopher half-whispered in Erica's direction.

"He was really uptight. You kids better stay away from him. I shouldn't even be telling you this. Don't you two belong in school now anyway?"

"It's recess," Erica said.

"We'll be careful," Cristopher assured him.

"Yeah, we will. And thanks," Erica replied.

"Do you know who he is or what he wants?" the young man asked.

"Yeah, we think we know," Cristopher replied, and he pressed his palm over the brooch in his pocket protectively. "But we really have to get back to school now. Thanks again."

"Yeah. Thanks again," Erica repeated, and the two of them turned and ran back toward school.

"Hey! Be careful now! You don't want to go messing with the likes of him," the man shouted at them.

When they rounded the bend, the front door of the school was in sight. Erica was just a few paces ahead of Cristopher when he heard the sound of an automobile engine behind them. He turned his head and spotted the gray car with the XYZ license plates bearing down from behind.

"Run faster, Erica!" Cristopher shouted.

Panting and out of breath, they reached the door, pulled it open, and practically dove into the shelter of the school building. Standing on their toes, they stared out the windows as the car drove past the circle, sped up the road, and disappeared.

CHAPTER 15

THE SECRET
IS REVEALED

"It seems it was not long after the Van Buren brooch disappeared that the business that made the family rich disappeared as well," Miss Shore began, as soon as all the kids were back in their seats. Cristopher and Erica seemed particularly out of breath, but Miss Shore just assumed that they had been playing tag or something out on the playground.

"In fact, it went bankrupt," she continued. "Mr. Van Buren, Jr. had been stealing money from his company for a long time in order to pay for the big houses and the yacht and the horses and everything else he had purchased over the years. He had also made some foolish investments and lost a lot of money gambling. It was his father, Cornelius Sr., who had made the family fortune, and it was Cornelius Jr. who lost it."

Miss Shore opened the folder with the copies she had made of the articles that Cristopher had brought in, and pulled out another old newspaper clipping. "Oddly, even though the insurance company paid a million dollars to Mr. Van Buren when the brooch was stolen, there were some suspicions about its disappearance. This article," she said as she held it up, "was in the local paper a few weeks later.

It seems that the insurance company had posted a reward for information leading to the recovery of the brooch. In the article, an unidentified source stated that he thought Mr. Van Buren himself had arranged the theft so that he could collect the insurance money!" Every pair of eyes was glued to the teacher's face.

"Apparently, the police could not find any evidence to support that claim, so they dropped the investigation. The entire episode remains a mystery to this day!" She passed around the article, but Cristopher could barely look at it. He quickly passed it to Erica, who just as quickly passed it to Hector.

"Does anyone have any questions or anything that they would like to contribute to this discussion?" Miss Shore asked the class. She looked directly at Cristopher and smiled. "Cristopher? Since this entire talk is the result of what you brought to class, would you like to add anything before we move on?"

Cristopher's heart was beating so hard that he thought everyone could probably see it right through his shirt. Finally, he nodded, and Miss Shore smiled as she saw that Erica was nodding her head as well.

"Well then?" she said.

Cristopher reached inside his pocket and carefully pulled out the pouch. He untied the string and stuck his thumb and index finger inside. He withdrew the brooch and held it up.

"We found it, Erica and I!" he said. "We found the Van Burens' stolen pin! We found the Jubilee Emerald!"

CHAPTER 16

THE POLICE PAY A VISIT

Cristopher's mom went to answer the doorbell. When she saw the police chief standing there, she was very concerned and pulled the door open as quickly as she could.

"Is everything all right, officer?" she asked anxiously.

"Yes, Missus. Not to worry," he replied. He called all the moms Missus and all the dads Mister. It was easier than remembering their names. "May I come in?"

"Of course. Would you like a cup of coffee? I just made a fresh pot," she said, but she was still worried, despite the chief's comment.

"No, thanks. I've had my quota for the day," he smiled.

"So what can I do for you?" she asked apprehensively.

"We were hoping that you could help us with a certain matter that we have been working on," the chief replied.

"I would be happy to, if I can. But why me?" she asked, surprised.

"A while ago you filed a report against a man that you said was snooping around your property. Here, let me show you his picture." The chief pulled a photograph from his shirt pocket.

"Why, yes, I did. He was definitely snooping around my

backyard," she explained. "You know, I saw him again recently, but I didn't say anything. Do you know who he is? Has he done something wrong?"

"More recently, your neighbor reported him trespassing. And it wasn't the first time. Apparently he has been seen in Albert's Cove on and off for a number of years now. Sporadically, you know. Mickey down at the service station called to tell me that he saw him a few times pumping gas and acting strangely. Now Mickey's not a gossip, you know, and he doesn't say things off the cuff."

"Go on," Cristopher's mom said.

"He told Mickey that his name was Payton Burney. But it is actually Cornelius Van Buren III. Do you recognize the name?"

"I most certainly do!" she said. "He must be the grandson of the man who built this house. This was the gatehouse to their estate many years ago."

"We ran his data through the crime unit computers and found some pretty unpleasant stuff. He certainly has a checkered past," the chief said. "The Feds sent a team down to his apartment in Florida with a search warrant. It seems he was involved in some insurance fraud a few years ago, and they were tipped off that some of the stolen merchandise might be in his place. When they searched his home, they came across this." The chief took a small bag out of another one of his pockets. "They sent it up here for us to examine." He pulled the string open and shook something out onto the table.

"The cameo!" Cristopher's mom blurted out.

"You know about this?" the chief asked surprised.

"Yes, as a matter of fact, I do," she said. She walked to the corner and opened the desk drawer. "Look at this!" she said. She showed the sheriff the picture of the stolen emerald with the cameo just visible in the background.

"Hmmm," the chief said. "Interesting. Very interesting. The

Feds were right. " He paused for a minute, like he was thinking hard. "We tested the pin so that we could tell how old it was, and look what we found," he said, as he pulled a photo from yet another pocket of his shirt. "Try looking at it with this." He offered her a small magnifying glass.

She bent over the photograph. It was a laboratory report of some kind that looked almost like an X-ray. There was a picture of the front and back of the cameo. Etched into the back of the stone were some microscopic letters.

"Read the piece of paper," the chief said. "It's what's written on the cameo. You couldn't see it with the naked eye. The forensics lab washed it in some kind of acid to remove the resin that filled in the etching. Then the lettering was clear. What's interesting, though, is that the resin was newly applied. He must have covered the writing himself so that no one else could stumble on the message. "

Cristopher's mom held the magnifying glass close to the page and read aloud:

*Find the statue with baby's face
that disappeared without a trace.
It's there your dreams will be fulfilled,
despite the cracks that can't be healed.*

"Hmm," she said to herself. "The statue with baby's face? Wait! I know what that means!" She almost screamed as all the pieces came together in her mind. "Follow me," she said, rushing out the back door, across the deck, and onto the back lawn—the police chief right at her heels.

She pushed her way through the bushes and stopped next to the fountain. The two of them stared at the little boy on top of the pedestal.

"Gosh, what happened here?" she exclaimed as she noticed the recent damage to the fountain and the statue. "It certainly

didn't look like this the last time I saw it, although that was quite a while ago. But that is most definitely the face on the cameo! Look at that half smile, and look at those ears!"

Broken tiles and debris were everywhere. "Looks like somebody else got here before we did," the chief said. He was just stepping over the edge of the fountain to take a look at the broken leg more closely when Cristopher's mom's cell phone rang.

"Hello?" she said after one ring. "I see. Oh, my! Yes. I understand. I do understand. Of course I will talk to him."

She was silent for a minute, nodding her head as if whoever she was talking to could see her.

"Yes, honey, I'm with the chief. The red-headed man? Yes, I remember. When? The diner? The drugstore, too? Of course! I will tell him immediately. You be careful now!" she finally said. She ended the call.

"That was my son," she said, as if he didn't already know. "He and his friend Erica are way ahead of us, it seems." The tension hung heavily in the air for another moment or so before she spoke again.

"Go on," the chief said anxiously.

"I think that you had better send some of your men to the airport right away," she said. "I believe that Cornelius Van Buren III is about to get on an AMI flight to Mexico!"

"Are you sure?" he asked her.

"My son told me he is. He said that he saw his ticket earlier, and that he's booked on the 5:30 flight. I don't know if Cristopher knows yet who he really is, but I would radio for help if I were you. And by the way, don't look for a redhead anymore. Cristopher said he probably dyed his hair black."

The chief pulled out his phone and hit speed dial.

CHAPTER 17

THE MYSTERY IS SOLVED

Erica and Cristopher sat quietly in the principal's office. They weren't sure if they were in a ton of trouble or not, but at least they felt safer here than they did yesterday in Cristopher's backyard—and way safer than they did a little while ago when that car almost caught up to them.

When Miss Shore realized that the brooch was real, she escorted Erica, Cristopher, and the brooch to the office. Cristopher was holding the black velvet pouch in his hand when Miss Whyte, the principal, walked in. They told her the whole story.

"How did you ever know where to look for it?" she finally asked.

"You just gotta learn to look at things closely sometimes before you pass them by," Cristopher said seriously, just like his mom would have said.

They stayed in the office for what seemed like hours. Every once in a while, Miss Whyte's assistant would poke her head in and smile at them in a funny way. Finally, Miss Shore walked in with their jackets and backpacks and told them to get ready to leave.

"Chief Collins will be here in a minute, and he'll drive the two of you back to your house, Cristopher," she said.

"Are we in trouble?" Cristopher asked, still uncertain.

"No, you are not," she replied gravely, but neither of them really believed her completely. Everybody was acting so strange and being so serious.

They stood up and followed her out the door. The whole school was standing and watching them, it seemed. Faces were pushed against all the glass doors, and the halls were lined with children and teachers. Even Mr. Samuels, the janitor, was peering at them from the door to the boiler room. Cristopher held on to the pouch as tightly as he could.

The chief said almost nothing the entire ride back. As the car turned down Cris's street, the police radio crackled.

"We got him, Chief!" they heard a voice say. "He was pretty surprised to see us waiting at security when he tried to go through. He walked right into our arms. Sure enough, he had a ticket to Mexico City. Great work!"

"Thanks," the chief replied. He turned around in his seat and gave Cristopher and Erica a thumbs-up.

Three minutes later, they pulled up to Cristopher's house. They could see a long black limousine parked in the very back of the driveway. Right next to it was the gray sedan with the XYZ license plates!

Cristopher nudged Erica with his elbow and signaled her with his eyes. "Look at that!" he whispered as he pointed warily at the gray car.

"Why is he here?" she asked.

"I guess we're gonna find out soon," Cristopher replied.

His parents came running out the front door when they saw the chief's car. Erica's mom was right beside them. Chief Collins got out and opened the back door, and the two kids climbed out.

"Hey, kiddo!" Cristopher's dad said as he slapped him on the back.

Cristopher turned away from looking at the cars and smiled back at him. "Hey, Pops," he said. He was happy that his dad was home.

Two men got out of the limousine and walked towards them. One carried a briefcase and looked very stern. At the same time, another much taller man climbed out of the gray sedan. The men from the limousine walked right up to Cristopher and Erica, and one reached out to shake their hands. They had no idea who he was, and his hand was big and cold, but they shook it anyway. Then he put his briefcase on the outstretched arms of the other man and opened it. He took out a folder and something that looked like a tiny telescope, he unfolded a velvet-lined board, and he laid it across the top of the case.

All this time, the man from the gray car just stood there, his hands clasped behind his back, not saying a word. Erica glanced at him. Despite the fact that he looked very grave, she thought he had a nice face. She smiled at him, and she was sure that he smiled back, even though his face got all serious again right away.

"If you would kindly hand me the Van Buren brooch," the man from the limousine said ceremoniously, and he reached out his hand once again.

Cristopher untied the string and pulled the top of the pouch apart. He took out the pin and handed it to the man, who put it on the velvet pad and held the scope against his eye. He bent in close and examined it carefully. Finally, he sighed deeply, folded the velvet pad around the brooch, and closed it up inside the briefcase.

"On behalf of the Guardsman Insurance Company of America, I would like to express our sincere appreciation for your invaluable assistance in finding this gem. I can assure you that as soon as the head office verifies its authenticity and authorizes payment, a substantial reward will be paid to each of you for recovering the Jubilee Emerald, which has been missing for over 50 years," he said.

Chief Collins stepped forward and whispered something in the insurance agents's ear.

"Ah, splendid," he replied, and turned his attention once again to Cristopher and Erica. "And thanks to you two, we have not only recovered the stone, but the chief has just informed me that we have captured Mr. Van Buren, too!"

Erica and Christopher looked at each other and smiled.

"My word!" Erica's mother said.

"Van Buren, Jr. had arranged to have the gem stolen by a common thief in order to collect on the insurance. The thief was to hide it in a statue of Van Buren's son that was originally part of the fountain in front of the old house. The thief did as he was asked, but Van Buren, Jr. had devised an elaborate plan to cover his tracks. He had the whole fountain, along with a number of other pools and statuary, dismantled in the middle of the night after the gem was hidden, and moved to different locations. The one statue of his son apparently ended up in what is now your backyard.

"Then he shuttered the mansion, and the whole family supposedly went to Palm Beach for the winter. They made a big deal about their departure, and took photographs and everything, I assume so that everyone would know they had left. Shortly thereafter, the entire house burned to the ground. Naturally, the thief who had stolen and hidden the emerald figured the gem was lost in the fire along with everything else," he explained. "The family, of course, collected payment on their fire insurance policy as well. "

"That's why the fountain wasn't in both pictures!" Erica said. But only Cris and the insurance agent knew what she was talking about.

"Yes, exactly," the man said. "But unfortunately for Van

Buren and fortunately for us, some of the workers he hired to move the statues didn't follow his directions very well. Our investigation of the records and work permits in the Village Hall eventually led us to the man who owned the company that Mr. Van Buren hired. It seems that when the workers he employed found out that the house had burned down, they got frightened. They were afraid that they could be traced, and they were in the country and working illegally at the time. They didn't want to be blamed for the fire, nor did they want anyone finding out that they were illegal aliens, so they made themselves scarce."

Cristopher looked at Erica and nodded knowingly. "That's why he went to talk to that guy's grandfather," he whispered to her. "He worked for that company."

"Afterwards, I imagine to his great frustration, Van Buren was unable to locate the movers and find out exactly where they'd put the statue," he continued. "The fox outfoxed himself in the end. The estate was huge—over 1,500 acres, with pastures for all the Black Angus steer they raised and horses they bred. It wouldn't have been easy to find without some idea of where it had been placed. Besides, the fire caused quite a stir back then, and there were reporters and curiosity seekers everywhere. Our insurance investigators were swarming all over the mansion and grounds as well, looking for clues to the fire as well as to the theft of that emerald."

Cristopher dug into his pocket and pulled out two crumpled photographs. The first was of the Van Buren family standing in front of the fountain with the mansion in the background. The second was almost the same, but the fountain was gone. He smoothed out the creases and handed them to his dad.

"That second picture is from that old folder we had down in the basement. How did everyone miss that all these years? I guess no one ever put the pictures side by side before now. Even if they did, I suppose it would have been hard to put two and two together," Cristopher's dad said, as he peered at the photos.

"It took us, the insurance investigators, and the FBI over 50 years to gather all of this information, and we still were not certain where the statue was," the chief said.

The man from the insurance company nodded and smiled at Cristopher and Erica.

"Van Buren etched a clue into the back of the cameo that he entrusted to his young son, Cornelius III, telling him which statue to look in when it was safe to do so—in case anything happened to him."

"And so the grandson has been searching for our fountain all these years," Cristopher's mom said. "And snooping around our house!" she added.

"Yes, that's correct," the man from the gray car said. Up until then, he had been completely silent. "I am Agent Fleming from the FBI. About a year ago, we stumbled upon the thief that Mr. Van Buren originally hired to do his dirty work."

"Awesome!" Cristopher whispered to Erica. "He's like a spy," he added about the FBI man.

"I knew he was on our side!" she replied proudly. "I had a feeling."

"Lucky for us, he had gotten himself involved in a new insurance scam with Guardsman, and this time he got caught," the insurance man added.

"We had no idea at first that he was involved in the Van Buren theft. But when our investigators began to interrogate him, he confessed to a number of crimes in hopes that if we recovered some of the stolen items, his charges might be reduced. Lo and behold, one of those crimes was the theft of the Jubilee Emerald," Agent Fleming explained.

"In exchange for the information, we agreed not to prosecute fully. He was an old man anyway," the insurance man said.

"Your police chief had received numerous reports in the past few years of a snooper in town. When you first reported him to the police many years ago," Agent Fleming said to Cristopher's parents, "we opened a file on him. That file has remained open all this time. When the chief started getting new complaints recently, he ran his records through the crime computers, and our people picked up the inquiries."

"For all these years, we at Guardsman never really believed that the gem was stolen. And since the jewel never surfaced, it was always on our radar," the insurance man added.

"We assumed that Van Buren was getting closer to locating the emerald when the complaints about him here started to increase," Agent Fleming said.

"He was the little boy in the picture," Cristopher said. "The one who looked so sad."

"Yes, he was," the insurance man said, and he sounded very impressed. "You should be a detective, young man. How did you know that?"

"He was gonna dye it black so that no one would recognize him," Cristopher said, and he pointed to the insurance man's head. "The last time we saw him, he was wearing a hat, too."

"The last time?" the man from the insurance company asked. "You mean you saw him more than once?"

"Yeah," Erica said. "We saw him a few days ago at the diner, but he had sunglasses on. He was mean to Cris."

"And I saw him looking into our backyard way long ago. We found some footprints in a flower bed by my house, and I think he was in our garage yesterday," Cristopher said to his mom and dad. "I bet he was the one who moved my dad's gloves out of the fountain. He just didn't know where to look for the emerald after we hid it again," Cristopher said, grinning at Erica. "Yesterday, he was at the drugstore when we went in to buy some comics, and just before he drove to the airport, he was talking to the grandson of the guy who used to be the gardener for the Van Buren estate."

"We knew he was going to try to get away then," Erica said proudly.

"Yeah, we found a boarding pass stub from his trip up here from Mexico City," Cristopher added. "Then we saw his return ticket at the drugstore."

"You can rest assured that he will not be bothering any of you again," Agent Fleming said. "He'll be spending some time behind bars. He's been stealing jewelry from his family's old society friends down in Palm Beach and fencing it. He'd already accepted a huge cash down payment from his black market fence for the Jubilee Emerald. He was starting to get pretty desperate."

"They wanted the stone that he'd promised them, or else they wanted their money back. He'd already lost the money gambling, and he was running out of time," the insurance man explained.

"No wonder he looked so nervous when he was talking on his cell," Cristopher said to Erica. "I bet they're in Miami, right?" he asked. Both men nodded.

"Our men are down there now rounding them up," Fleming replied. "I have been watching Van Buren closely for the past few days, but when you waved to me at the drugstore, I realized that my cover might have been blown. If you found me out so easily, I thought maybe he would, too. So I was planning to switch cars.

"First, though, I followed him to your school. After he got back in his car, he was in quite a hurry. I figured that he finally decided it was time to run. That's when I passed you kids racing up the road. I thought we were going to lose him for a minute there. Sorry if I scared you," he said sympathetically.

Cristopher and Erica looked at each other and grinned. They were glad they'd found the emerald, and they were even happier knowing that no strange men would be snooping around anymore when they were on an adventure.

"Dad?" Cristopher turned to his father. "Do you think Erica and I can use some of our reward money to take us all on a trip?

You know, like, a real vacation?"

"Well, that sounds like a very generous offer, Cris. Where would you two like to go?" he replied.

Cristopher looked at Erica, and they appeared to be thinking very seriously about his question.

"Hey, I know!" Cristopher finally replied. "How about Mexico?"